NO *perfect* WOMAN

IMPERFECTION SERIES BOOK 5

Award-winning Author
DD LORENZO

To my readers.
Thank you for waiting on Marisol's story.
Her book is supposed to be the final in the series.
You be the judge.
I'll listen for the verdict.

Prologue

Marisol

On nights like this, I wondered if anything I could have done differently would have changed the outcome of this circumstance. Many nights the black of a midnight sky stole my sleep and flooded my veins with the murky tar of speculation. My thoughts tortured me, giving me no rest from my endless pondering of what could have been—what should have been. What I did know for sure was that my love for her had energized me, fueling me to be the best version of myself, and I'd failed her miserably. I didn't deserve her. She was, and would always be, the impetus that drove me to be the best—for her.

Love had made me a better person, and my love for her allowed me to live happily with myself in blissful ignorance, though I couldn't erase the sins from my past. Even though her sweetness blessed me with an inner light I'd never experienced, no matter how I tried I couldn't wash the condemnation from my soul. I would have spent every day for the remainder of my life seeking absolution if it would have meant I could have kept her forever. Since that would never happen, I'd have to be satisfied with holding her in my heart.

It was either a travesty or fitting justice that I might never be healed by the sweetness of her forgiveness.

Chapter 1

Marisol

I*t's finished!*

There was something decadent about perfection, and I was looking at it. A nursery that was fit for a princess. Our princess. I still had to get used to the idea I was going to be a mother, but it pleased Manny that I was directing my attention to decorating the nursery. All of my plans had turned into reality, just as I'd pictured them in my mind. The room was filled with color. Unimaginable hues of pink mixed with smatterings of coral, yellow, and white. The walls were painted in such a way the colors graduated seamlessly and beautifully, one into the other. The illusion it created was of the morning sunrise in Bogota.

The slight smile on my face was genuine, and

though I would have thought otherwise, I was happy to be home. Manny and I had returned home from the United States, our sights set on reigning in the political arena. The first step, become a real family.

As my gaze traveled from one pretty thing to another, I imagined that some would argue the decor was excessive. I wouldn't agree, nor did I care. This was our child. Though I didn't intend to be a mother in the traditional sense of the word, I planned to lavish this child with the best of everything for appearances' sake.

A wave of exhaustion lingered over me. Manny and I had been traveling extensively. Our social activities were each planned with our goals in mind. The night before we'd hosted a dinner party for fifty guests. The elite of Colombian society. Most of the attendees were influential in the social circles in this country and abroad. Manny and I spared no expense when we entertained, taking necessary steps to assure our victory when the time came. We were both well aware that presenting ourselves as a stable family would further our ambition, so it was decided we would add a child to our family.

At first, I was adamantly opposed to the idea, after all, many political couples were childless. Manny didn't care and convinced me by threatening to exercise his guardianship if I didn't comply. When I argued that he couldn't do that without notice, he said that people would understand that I was overwhelmed, and he would explain that I needed to go away to a facility for "rest." We battled, but I had no choice. Adding a child to our home was the condition for my so-called freedom.

Accepting that I would be playing the mother role took some time. I possessed no maternal instincts. I didn't like children, they were messy and noisy. Manny's threatening reminders only served to convince me my outlook would have to change because the stakes were high. I consented, agreeing to put on a united front. What choice did I have?

It was decided that last night's event would be my last. Should there be questions, Manny would explain that I was preparing for the impending arrival. In time, Manny and I would reemerge with our little one. Though I wasn't happy about the baby's arrival, I looked forward to the warm reception of the public. It would be a welcome change after the negative publicity I'd received.

Today was the first I was able to sit back and enjoy my efforts. I'd told Manny that if I had to like this kid, nothing would be too good for it. People would be watching, and I wanted to provide the best that money could buy. Any child would love this room, and since I didn't plan on spending much time with the child, I provided a space where it couldn't help but be happy. The results were stunning.

I imagined this room would set the bar for designers specializing in child décor. Built-in bookshelves were full of children's stories. A tiny dressing room, mimicking my own, was off to the right of the crib. It would photograph well should Manny decide to let journalists in to take a look. I took the few steps necessary toward the overstuffed rocking chair. It was powder blue and hugged my frame perfectly as I leaned back into it. A miniature crystal chandelier hung in the center, just over a changing table. It was filled with diapers, powder, and lotions. One wall held racks of tiny shoes, and the closet rods were filled with outfits from the world's best designers. To the world, the child of Manny and Marisol Vallega would appear pampered and spoiled, but, of course, appearances can be deceiving.

The media painted a picture of our lives with a broad brush. Because of my bipolar diagnosis, Manny insisted that I be the face of his philanthropic efforts in the area of mental health diseases and disorders. Within a short period, his goodwill efforts toward emotional illness and generous contributions paid off. He shed the shadow of his association with my father and instead became the poster boy of change. His drive and ambition were respectable enough that he announced that his sights were set on the presidency of Colombia. The harsh spotlight on us had softened as the result of our efforts, and the public focus became more positive than negative. No longer were we seen as two isolated people, and now we were delighted, expectant parents. Through the power of the media and planned photo ops, we became more respectable, and public opinion was rising.

I found it strange how a child could sway public perception, but Manny didn't. Nothing was off-limits for him to get what he wanted. A child's life was but one price to pay.

Chapter 2

"I thought I'd find you here." The deep timbre of Manny's voice resonated throughout the suite. The tone was thick and creamy and, despite my resistance, sent a shiver down my spine. I didn't like that he had this effect on me. Sex was a weapon I'd honed into a sharp blade, and it had served me well. Though I tried not to be attracted to him, something primal inside of me was drawn to him. My back arched when he came behind me, his hot breath caressing my neck as he kissed the hollow beneath my ear. I turned toward him, a contented smile playing at the corners of my lips.

"I was inspecting the finishing touches." I looked up at the chandelier. "Stunning, isn't it?"

He followed the direction of my gaze. "Very nice. I'm glad to see you embracing your new role."

Although I was a woman of considerable height,

Manny stood taller than me. Everything about him screamed male. His broad, tight chest showcased his bronzed skin. His cheekbones framed the hollow space leading to a stern, square jawline. His lips were full and thick and velvety. But it was Manny's eyes that were my undoing. They were magnetic with thick, black lashes, sucking me into the compliance of a sex slave. The brown pools bordered near black. If his life had followed the same path as mine, he would have made a killing in the modeling industry. I licked my lips as my gaze traveled to his trim waist. It was adorned by a simple black leather belt, but I knew what was hidden beneath his slacks; a tight ass, powerful thighs, and strong legs. Manny's physique was a credit to his sex. Everything about him defined masculinity, and any woman would thrill to have him between her legs. I was sure many had.

He leaned down, his lips scorching my ear. I could almost smell his desire. I hated him but loved how he made me feel. As I leaned into him, I felt his chest expand with a deep inhale. "Mmm. That's a familiar scent."

He pulled me back against him and closed his arms around me. "You bought it for me."

"I know. I like it." We stood in front of a full-length mirror. Manny studied me. "You appear happy, Marianna. It looks good on you."

"I am as happy as I can be." I waved my hand at the

scene before us. "After all, who wouldn't be happy surrounded by all of these pretty things."

He squeezed me a little tighter, pressing his erection against my backside. "I think impending motherhood agrees with you."

His tone was thick with desire. Manny's use of my given name filled my core with heat, a feeling I tried to fight. Only he called me Marianna. No one else would dare use my real name. My mother and father were dead, as was my twin. My two brothers were killed in cartel-related business, and my other sisters were married. I hadn't seen them for years, and when I did, I insisted they use my professional name. To the world, I was Marisol Franzi Vallega. To Manny, I was Marianna—*his* Marianna.

I scoffed as I turned my head, giving him a sideways glance as I narrowed my eyes. Amusement danced in my words. "I don't know that motherhood will change me. I've always been delightful."

His laugh was genuine, unmasked by the propriety he presented in business. He tapped his finger against my lips. "You are delightful. And you're mine." His hand brushed over my stomach.

I didn't respond, though he was correct. As much as I detested it, Manny understood me in ways no one else ever could. Our roots were cultivated in the same rotten soil, yet here we were, thriving. I allowed myself a moment of satisfaction to feel the familiar rush of desire that only he could rouse. There was no denying our mutual attraction. He was freakishly intuitive with my many moods. Still, I didn't want to give in. My pride still smarted because this baby had been forced on me. I attempted to change the subject as I looked around the room.

"Do you think we've forgotten anything?" I broke our embrace, stepping away to collect myself.

He placed his hand in his pocket. A condescending look veiled his eyes. "I don't think you would take the chance of disappointing me, but if you are looking for a compliment, I can only say that you are unequaled when it comes to décor, my dear. No one would dare question your taste. It is impeccable and nothing less than I expected."

I tried to mask how much the comment pleased me. "You might be interested to know that a home décor magazine approached the designer I've been working with. They have expressed a desire to feature our nursery in their May issue."

He stared at me, a scowl furrowing his brow as his lips tightened into a thin line. "No."

I craved the spotlight once again, even if it was for something as stupid as a nursery. "You should reconsider that position. It could be good for our image." Though my tone begged him to rethink his position, his gaze hardened.

"I said no, Marianna. Absolutely not. No photographs. There are too many unknowns at this time with the child. For security reasons, I forbid it.

This is the only place where I dictate our privacy. Our home is off-limits to the press."

I turned to him, my fingers playing at the lapels on his jacket. I had put much time and effort into this room and I wanted recognition. I looked into his eyes. "It's a very prestigious publication. Reconsider." I pressed my lips to him in a gentle kiss.

He returned my gaze with a hardened one. I knew this expression well, yet it was in my nature to push the limits of his patience.

"I give in to you more than I should, Marianna. Perhaps you don't remember that we do things my way or not at all. I said no. I do not expect to be challenged again. Do you understand?"

I nodded as I ran a finger down his zipper. "You can be so—"

In a heartbeat, he placed a hand over my mouth and grabbed a fistful of my hair. He demanded my silence, a wicked grin hooking one corner of his mouth. "So what, Marianna? Kind? Thoughtful? Giving?"

His voice dropped an octave, caressing the hidden threat in his words. Secretly, I loved his response when I pushed him. No one did that. No one else would dare.

He raised a questioning brow. "Answer me."

"You are all of those things, and so much more, *mi amor*."

His grip tightened, stinging my scalp. An ominous chuckle resonated deep within his chest. "You think you know me, don't you, *chica?*" He pushed me back, pinning me between the wall and his chest. "I assure you, you don't."

He gave my hair a harsh yank, exposing my neck, baring his teeth against my skin. I fought him, stiffening my spine as I pushed him away, but I was no match for my husband. His nips against my tender flesh were quick and sharp. He never bit deep enough to leave a mark, just enough to remind me that I craved the pain. Manny's touch wasn't tender and loving, it was forceful and demanding. I despised Manny, but sex was a different matter. I loved it—and he knew it.

I'd barely caught my breath when he spun me around. Crushing me into the wall, my breasts and belly stung as they suffered against the freshly covered surface. He hiked up my skirt, making quick work of removing my panties as he ripped them off in one vicious tug. I sucked in a breath.

"You will obey me." He thrust his hand between my legs and my body flooded with lust. His touch seared my skin, electrifying it as he moved his fingers in hard circles. I defied him, pushing back against him with my ass. This only excited him further.

In a quick motion, he kicked my legs apart. I was hot and wet with desire. I shivered as cool air brushed against my heat, an involuntary shudder betrayed my feelings. Manny placed his lips to my ear.

"Cat got your tongue, my love?" The cynicism in his tone combined with the hushed sound of a lowering zipper filled the momentary silence. Manny grabbed my wrists, slamming my hands against the wall as he willed me immobile. A beastly tone saturated his order. "Don't move."

I refused to listen and tried to buck away from him. In response, he flipped my skirt up around my waist and gripped my hips with both hands. I barely had time to catch a breath before his cock torpedoed into me. He thrust straight and hard between my legs. There was no way to escape. I was no match for his strength, yet, still, I defied him, jerking my ass in awkward motions. My resistance was met with a full slap on my cheek.

"You know you crave this. You will do as I say, Marianna. You answer to me!"

His words laced with my lust, knotting us into a twisted union. He took what he wanted, ruthless in his invasion. Removing a hand from my hip, he strummed me with his fingers.

My body betrayed me. My cravings for him assaulting any rational thoughts as I submitted to his will.

There was no way to break our connection, but then, I had no desire to do so. With quick, powerful precision, Manny slammed his cock into me over and over. I no longer had any choice but to give in because his animalistic cravings mimicked my own. He sank his teeth into my shoulder as he pounded into my blistering core. I cried out as my thoughts swam in a frenzy. Rocking against him, I begged for relief. There was no point in denying how Manny made me feel. Over and over he claimed me until I exploded. He shuddered as he emptied himself inside me, marking me as his once again.

A few minutes later I opened my eyes, reorienting myself with my surroundings. Manny had pulled himself out of me and bent over to retrieve what was left of my panties. He wrapped them around his cock, wiping away the evidence of what had just transpired, then tossing the garment into a waste can. Sexual satisfaction betrayed my loathsome feelings for the man himself, bringing on mutinous thoughts. No one had ever satisfied me the way Manny did, and I hated my body for its unholy desire.

I slid my hands down the wall to gain leverage, tingles in my fingers and palms appearing as blood rushed back into them. I pushed myself away from the wall, my skirt still around my waist, my thighs wet and sticky. A sinister chuckle met my ears as Manny's open palm made a cracking sound as it met my ass cheek.

"Straighten yourself, Marianna. It's time for dinner."

Chapter 3

The control that Manny wielded over me made me hate him.

Unclenching my muscles, I stiffened my spine. I would play to Manny's need for control for as long as necessary. I didn't have much choice, but time would become my friend as I learned to beat him at his own game. His rules were simple, do as he said, or lose my freedom.

Despite my efforts to stay away from men like my father, I was now imprisoned by one. Manny possessed the same personality traits. Papi had never been an affectionate man. Instead, he'd preyed on the weaknesses of others. He'd been ruthless, taking whatever he wanted, never asking.

He and Manny shared those characteristics, yet to fool others there were times when Manny doled out affection. In social settings, where most men preferred to keep their public displays to a minimum, Manny played the doting husband. He held my hand or placed his at the small of my back. What others thought endearing was, instead, a tether of control. To survive this marriage, I couldn't believe any illusion of care or concern. Manny's goal was to create a persona as an upstanding citizen, doting husband, and loving father. This much I knew, people were gullible.

What he didn't realize was how much more powerful I'd become. Relinquishing my body was a small price to pay for sharpening my hatred. Love was useless, but hate made you dig deep inside of yourself for survival. I retraced my every encounter with Manny, sexual and otherwise. I ingested them, digested the lessons I learned, and let the knowledge it gave me ricochet from my head to my heart. Both were learning to be finely tuned, precision instruments of my will. I would break free, and I vowed that, when I did, no one would ever use me again.

There was only one thing that I appreciated about Manny—his power. In that regard he and I were alike. There were times when I wondered what true affection and love would feel like, but whenever I found myself weakening to tender thoughts, I immediately shut it down. Loving someone was a weakness.

Manny possessed what I wanted—power; it was his drug. I was the wife of one of the worlds most feared men and, like an addict, I wanted what he had. In the society of the underworld there was an understood hierarchy. No one would dare deny me anything I wanted because of my connections. Manny walked the line between respect and contempt. He had worked hard for an influential position, yet still controlled the cartel. He masterfully distanced himself between the two, but if I so chose, I could use all that I knew to take him down.

Teresa entered the room. I was naked from the waist down, having stepped out of my disheveled clothes. She saw everything but said nothing. I had trained her well. She knew where to place her loyalty, and I rewarded her handsomely for the privilege of assisting me. She held out two skirts, having anticipated my need.

"The one on the left." My tone was clipped. Minutes ticked away, and it wouldn't be long until Manny sent someone for me. Teresa removed the garment from its hangar. I slipped out of my shoes and into my freshly cleaned and pressed selection. The only thing that made life bearable was knowing how much it would change when Manny became president.

A surprising warmth flooded me as I pictured myself the first lady of Colombia. It comforted my bruised ego knowing the time would come when I could have anything I wanted because of him. I could play the part of the dutiful wife, my compliance feeding Manny's need to control. It was all really part of an agenda hidden deep inside of me, unseating the King of Corruption.

My jaw anchored as I looked myself over in the full-length mirror. No one controlled me. Not Manny and not this little brat that had been forced upon me. I raised my chin defiantly and then smoothed back my hair, all while biting back the urge to march into the dining room and tell him to shove his plans up his self-righteous ass. Though it was a pleasant thought, I pushed it away. He didn't know it, but he was laying the groundwork for his own undoing, and the child he wanted so badly would play a pivotal role.

Chapter 4

"You're late." Manny dabbed his napkin at the corner of his mouth.

"I wasn't appropriately dressed for dinner. I had to make myself presentable." Sarcasm saturated my words as they dripped off my tongue. As I took a seat at the table, I noted a smug smile played at the corner of his mouth. It was almost painful to bite back the words I wanted to say to him, as my instinctual rebellion simmered in my belly. His egotistical, satisfied look coaxed it to buck free. If I did, all hell would break loose, ending with Manny's constant threats to send me away for a "rest." I held my tongue because he held all the cards at the moment, but it wouldn't always be that way.

He tossed the napkin onto his plate. "I'll be leaving within the hour," Manny told me with a smile. "I'm flying out tonight. I've sent Miguel to pack for me."

"Where are you going?" He tilted his head to the side. A cocked eyebrow told me he'd misread the lilt in my voice as missing him when, in fact, I was looking forward to being free of him.

"Why, Marianna. You sound as if you'll miss me."

I said nothing. Let Manny believe what he wanted to believe, I merely wanted to keep tabs on his whereabouts.

I smiled at him as he rose from the table and approached me. He kissed my head.

"It's so nice to know you care."

I stiffened. "You didn't answer my question."

"I'm flying to the States." He cupped my chin, forcing me to look at him. He would be disappointed if he was waiting for a reaction. I had none, other than that of a dutiful wife. The muscles in my jaw burned as I grappled to secure my smile, so much so it felt as though my back teeth would break from clenching. "I have a meeting with Senator Bushman. He's one of the president's closest allies. He has set up a meeting for the three of us."

"Did you know this earlier today?"

"No more questions, Marianna," he chided. "This will be a good opportunity for you to rest before assuming your motherly duties." Manny stayed where he was while my dinner was placed before me. "Eat, then I think you should retire for the evening. You look tired."

I had no appetite. He knew I yearned to return to

the States, yet his invitation to accompany him never came. This was his third trip there in as many months, and he'd refused to take me with him each time. I sometimes wondered if I would ever get back to New York and my condo.

"Is something wrong?"

Though I didn't show it on the outside, he detected my mood. His response was clipped and severe. I looked up at him, plastering on my sweetest smile. "Not at all. I think you're right. I may turn in early tonight."

"I'll see you before I leave."

As Manny left the room, I played with the food on my plate. Damn him! He knew how badly I wanted to shun his never-ending list of duties and have some fun, yet he refused to indulge me. He wielded his authority over me, having been named my guardian as required when I was released from the Perkins facility in Maryland. He'd lured me back to Colombia with promises of a better life with him. He thought I was fragile; I was anything but. What he read as a delicate constitution was really my ability to mask my bitterness. He'd painted a grand picture of our life together, describing for me the compound that was to be our home. He'd taken the house I'd grown up in and added a massive expansion. He'd given me free rein to decorate it however I wanted, but, being the control freak he was, he'd had the final say on every decision I made. Hell, he even instructed the servants as to what time of day the curtains would be opened. If Manny could have controlled the sun, he would have picked a time when he wanted the light to filter into the rooms.

Life with Manny was like living under a microscope. In my absence, Manny had developed into much more of a dictator than my father had ever been. He sensed my unhappiness but didn't care. I was more a prisoner than a wife. Once, just to keep me off balance, he'd surprised me by asking me to accompany him to Las Vegas. Though I'd welcomed getting away, our trip had not gone as planned.

Mistakenly, I'd thought that while Manny had his meetings, I'd be left alone with access to my bank account and credit cards. I'd been itching to indulge myself within the walls of Cartier, Givenchy, and Alexander McQueen. Instead, he'd given me his credit card and a bodyguard to monitor my every move. It was apparent he didn't trust me, but, then, I believed him even less.

Manny'd been unaware of my accounts, and to secure my freedom, I'd needed to access them. All it would have taken were a few disposable phones to make calls he couldn't monitor.

I'd tried my best to get away from the man accompanying me as I shopped, but he'd stayed close. Being dragged through store after store, he'd started to get bored. Eventually, he'd waited outside at the door as I took my time. Finally, I'd found a way to break free when one store connected to another through the back end. I slipped out the second door when the crowd was thick and made a quick exit from the building.

Knowing it wouldn't take long for the man to realize I was gone, I'd left the Strip, turning down a side street. I had no idea where I was going, but I knew I could purchase cell phones at any drug store. I could buy one, transfer funds, and then get a ride back to the hotel. I'd thought I had everything under control when I found a store to make the purchases. Once outside, I'd made my call and threw the phone away. I'd purchased two others and they were lying at the bottom of my bag. All I'd needed to do was hail a taxi and perfect my cover story. I'd walked down a side street to do just that, but something more sinister than escapes and telephone calls awaited me.

I'd heard a clanging noise and caught a glimpse of a rolling, metal trash can. Blood was everywhere, and Blake Matthews was the source. I'd tucked myself into a doorway with an unobscured view as one of Manny's men took off. Though I hadn't know him personally, I recognized him as one of the men who frequented our Colombian home. As he'd run in one direction, I heard yelling from the opposite one and saw Falcon Gray running toward the scene. I'd looked down again at Blake and saw Paige Kasey on the ground as well. I'd gotten away as fast as I could, running to find any open door. I'd been terrified that, if my presence were detected, I'd somehow be connected. That was the last thing I'd needed.

When I'd returned to the hotel that night, it had taken everything in me to behave nonchalantly, all the while knowing my husband had been responsible for the fates of Blake and Paige.

Now, as then, I struggled to keep my breathing even. I silently counted to ten as oxygen filtered through my lungs. I reached up my hand and, in a tender motion, placed my palm against my husband's cheek. "Have a safe trip, my love. I'll see you when you return."

His gentle smile indicated the endearment pleased him when, in truth, I'd rather have slapped his face than caress it.

WITH MANNY GONE from the house, I returned to the nursery. Though I didn't eagerly anticipate the new role I must adopt, I still had a strong sense of pride. Appearance was everything, and this child would be a reflection of my position as a mother. Any indication that I was inadequate was unacceptable. To anyone watching I would be a perfect parent.

The nursery was housed on the garden side of the mansion. The suite was large and sat on the corner of the structure. I had positioned the rocker in that corner, knowing that a glance to my left was filled with beautiful flowers. Bright reds, yellows, and differing shades of white gently dressed the crisp green colors of the lawn and bushes. The scene was relaxing in both sunshine and rain. But the view to my right was the perfect angle to spy vehicles coming and going. It was my only way to see when Manny, and others, entered and exited the mansion. Manny never questioned me when I selected this space for the nursery, and I never offered an explanation.

He kept me as a gilded bird, and, as such, I watched from my perch as Manny left the premises.

I walked into the dressing room area, scanning the racks of clothing for the child's first outfit, but, really, I was perfecting a diversion for something more calculated than picking out clothes. There were still people here who'd been loyal to my father and hated that Manny was his successor. Because of their feelings, they'd secretly approached me and offered their support.

I took it. Even little birdies had their secrets.

Chapter 5

I retired to the sitting room that adjoined the master bedroom. Manny hadn't been away from the house for five minutes when my cell phone rang. I hit the receive button. "Yes, Manny."

"I gave Teresa instructions before I left the house. I believe that you need rest, my dear. She will assure that you get it. I've told her no calls or visitors for you while I'm away."

A veiled order was still an order and indignation raised the hairs on the back of my neck. "Of course. I wouldn't have it any other way."

"I'll call you when I arrive in Washington."

I breathed a sigh of relief as the call ended. I was happy to be free of Manny, even for a short time.

Manny and I served each other's purposes. Publicly and privately we appeared to have a healthy marriage. I would be lying to myself if I said he didn't attract me sexually. He was a skilled lover, and I took everything he gave, but, then, sex wasn't everything. Survival was of greater importance to me. I was under no illusion that Manny loved me. If my death would further his agenda, he would surely find a creative way for me to die. But Manny needed me to play the part of loving mother. The child would need me as much as I needed it. Both of us would play a role in a scripted life, but we would have to rely on each other so neither of us became dispensable. This mindset inspired me to protect myself.

Satisfied Manny would be gone for a while, I returned to the nursery and went into the baby's dressing area. Approaching the wall that held numerous pairs of tiny shoes, I looked over my shoulder. Once assured I was alone, I ran my hand down the molding on the right until I felt a small, metal lever. I applied pressure, and a door opened. Inside was a bathroom complete with shower.

Manny didn't know I'd put a bathroom in the nursery. It wasn't on the original blueprint for the renovation. Should he find it and question me about it I planned to say it was part of Teresa's new quarters and was connected to her au pair suite. It was understood that she would be spending most of her time with the baby once it arrived. The only reason for the access through the dressing room was for my convenience, should I have the need to use the restroom—or escape.

I walked to the small closet and in a few easy steps

pulled the entire cabinet away from the wall to reveal a large panic room. It was completely hidden from prying eyes. Also hidden in the design blueprint was an elevator designed to fit one person. It went directly from this room to a hidden area on the ground floor and could be locked on either end.

One wall of the panic room was filled with monitors showing differing spaces both inside and outside the house. I'd enlisted the aid of those who'd risked their lives by offering me their loyalty above any they had to Manny. I'd accepted their support, telling them I needed people I could trust to guard my baby. I demanded their confidence; it was a prerequisite of any offer to work for me. Most had no suspicions I was anything other than an overprotective mother. They were well aware Manny had security throughout the compound but accepted that I wanted additional protection for the baby. Since they were house staff, Teresa had privately relayed to them that Manny would be upset if he knew about the room and would take my lack of confidence in his security measures personally. No one wanted to subject me to Manny's temper and, because of their loyalty to me, agreed to keep my secret. I suspected that they, too, had reasons to not trust Manny, but none they shared with me. I stepped inside the panic room where Teresa was waiting.

"He is gone, señora."

"Yes, I watched him leave. Thank you, Teresa." I

walked over to my assistant of many years and placed my hand on her shoulder. "Would you please get me some tea and something light to eat? I didn't eat my dinner."

She nodded, gave me a slight smile, and then turned away. I'd mellowed toward her over the years. I'd known Teresa since my tenth birthday. My mother had assigned her to my sisters and me as a type of nanny and housekeeper. Over the years she'd put up with much, especially my many moods. But it was imperative I had someone close who thought about my safety above their own, and Teresa was that person. Her loyalty to me was without question and, of all the people in my world, she was the closest to me.

I'd designed the three rooms next to the nursery as an au pair suite. Though it was for Teresa to live in, it could provide me an escape from my husband. Manny and I were oil and water. We tolerated each other only for the common good. I hoped that when the baby arrived, it would provide the excuse I needed to spend most of my leisure time away from him and in this part of the house. Manny always had the final say as to how I kept my schedule—and I hated it. If I stuck close to the nursery, the panic room would provide a safe space should any cartel business get out of hand.

I looked around, pleased with the design and operation. Roberto sat inside. He always entered the panic room via the hidden elevator, raising no suspicion of his comings and goings from the other household staff.

He sat at a plain, but functional, black desk. The lines of the furniture were sleek and modern compared to what I'd chosen for the rest of the house. The room was reinforced so that if I locked it from the inside, no one could open it from the outside.

"Did you get all of the footage from the nursery this afternoon?" Though I wasn't embarrassed at all that this man had witnessed my husband's demand for sex, the barrel-chested man looked embarrassed by the question.

"Sí, señora."

A flush of color appeared around his collar. Apparently, videotaping and recording his employers fucking wasn't something he anticipated.

"Good. Keep the footage. We never know when I'll need it."

There was always something lurking in the shadows, and his duties would evolve as time passed by. I knew all too well that danger was only a gun, knife, or bomb away. I intended to protect myself from all threats, including any from my husband.

Chapter 6

M anny

Due to nasty weather, the flight took nearly six hours. Nonetheless, Manny and Miguel had arrived safely in Washington, D.C. Not wishing to draw attention to himself, Manny had refused the senator's offer to send a car and, instead, had Miguel secure one for them. The meeting was to take place at the infamous Watergate hotel. Manny hoped the senator had the good sense to check the room for recording devices and made a mental note to ask him.

Manny and Miguel stepped off the elevator and into a private suite. The décor was a mix of whites and grays, with a lack of depth or clean lines in any of the furniture. It was precisely the type of thing he'd expect of the capitol of the United States—cold and sterile.

"Ah, Manny." Senator Bushman approached with an outstretched hand. "Good to see you." He eyed the other man. "You didn't tell me that you were bringing a guest."

"This is my personal assistant, Miguel." He tipped his head between the two men. "Miguel, Senator William Bushman."

Miguel reached out to shake the senator's hand, then stepped back into place beside his boss. The senator raised a questioning eyebrow at Manny.

"If you're concerned about Miguel's trustworthiness, let me assure you he will not repeat a word we discuss."

"I'm confident you believe so, but we can't be too careful. Confidentiality is important." Manny detected his hesitancy to believe Manny's statement as truth, and it didn't sit well with him.

"Again, let me assure you that my assistant will not speak a word of what he hears. He knows that otherwise, I will cut out his tongue."

Shock registered on Bushman's face, but he quickly regained his composure. He slapped Manny on the shoulder.

"Perhaps we should all threaten our assistants with the same," the senator laughed. Manny and Miguel were not amused.

"Is the president here?" Manny asked.

"Yes. They're all waiting. Come with me."

All? Manny silently questioned the term as he walked alongside Bushman. It was his understanding that it was a three-person meeting. Miguel trailed a few steps behind. Bushman was a crucial player in his plans. He was weak, pliable, and arrogant enough to believe he was indispensable. Though elected, he had much to learn about politics. Fortunately, all of those issues worked in Manny's favor. The senator was willing to turn a blind eye to just about anything in exchange for an account full of untraceable cash to fund his more undesirable and secret habits.

The sound of their footsteps was muffled on the thick carpet. Miguel was still a step behind. Neither man was armed, but Miguel had been trained in martial arts and wouldn't hesitate to protect Manny.

As they approached the makeshift conference room, Manny pulled on the shirt sleeves beneath his jacket. Another man was exchanging conversation with the man Manny recognized as the President of the United States. While the president stayed seated, the other man stood.

"Manny." Before him with an outstretched hand, was a politician he knew much about but hadn't yet met in person. Senator Ford's greeting seemed too familiar for a first meeting, but men like this one always took liberties. Manny was aware that this particular senior politician had corruption in his heart. At the top of the list was his abhorrent appetite for young boys.

"Senator. So nice to meet you in person. Your reputation precedes you." Manny returned the man's handshake, noting with disgust his sweaty palm.

"Mr. President." Manny extended a hand. The president remained seated, casually ignoring the offered hand and motioning for everyone to take a seat.

"Now that the introductions are out of the way . . ." The president's tone was impatient. "Let's get down to business. I hear you need a little help getting elected, Manny. Why should I help you?"

It was perfectly clear to Manny why most people thought this man arrogant. He possessed very little diplomacy but a lot of balls.

"I can't answer that for you, Mr. President, but know that should I win the presidency of my country, you would have an ally in Colombia."

Manny could tell the man's interest was piqued, but Senator Ford's face was a study in skepticism.

"I don't believe there's anything your country can do for us, Mr. Vallega. The United States can hold its own."

Manny wanted to knock the smug look off the older man's face. "With all due respect, Senator Ford, everyone can use friends—even the United States."

"I have plenty of friends!" Senator Ford gave a knowing look to the president, and the two laughed at their private joke. Irritation prickled the hairs on Manny's neck.

"I'm sure you do, Senator Ford. Especially those who supply your little . . . habit."

The laughing ceased as all attention quickly turned to Manny.

"Correct me if I'm wrong, Senator, but doesn't your brother own Cyclops Transport?"

Senator Ford's posture stiffened, and his eyes narrowed. "My brother's business dealings are his own, Mr. Vallega. I have nothing to do with his company."

"I beg to differ." Miguel handed Manny a sheet of paper, he, in turn, handed it to the man.

"This is an email correspondence between you and your brother on Friday, the thirteenth of July. It seems you were unhappy with the merchandise delivered to you at one of your residences in Pennsylvania. In your words, "they were dehydrated and sick." I wonder what your constituents would think of their Senator and his brother importing human cargo?"

The Senator's face flushed with anger and his tone held a threat. "You can't—"

"But I can," Manny interrupted. "I have no interest in your proclivities. As a businessman, I simply ask that you don't trivialize my position. After all, I'm only a man who is concerned with doing what's right for his country."

A hush fell over the room and, for a moment, it was deathly quiet.

"Senator—or should I call you Ed since it seems we're on a first name basis?" Manny chided. "Let me make myself clear. My plans have nothing to do with you or your brother, but, make no mistake, if you try to thwart my efforts toward the presidency of Colombia, I would have to make this email, and many others, public. You may not know this, but my country has quickly growing, vast information technology industry. We find new ways every day to navigate the many layers of various means of telecommunications.

"Although I know you aren't publicly affiliated in any way that could lead to being accused of coercion, I am aware you have invested in some companies that would compromise your reputation. I think your influence could help me, just as I know mine could hurt you. I do, however, believe we can be gentlemen about this. Wouldn't you agree?"

A thin line of perspiration had formed on Senator Ford's upper lip.

"So, then, Ed," Manny continued, "do we have an agreement?"

Chapter 7

Manny Senator Ford eyed Manny suspiciously, while the younger Senator Bushman seemed to be holding his breath. The president, on the other hand, leaned back in his chair, his countenance awash with amusement as he watched the scene unfold. Finally, Senator Ford broke the tension. He clapped a hand on Manny's shoulder.

"I see a natural born politician in you, Vallega! You'll go far." His words danced on his laughter. He looked at the president. "Good man, here! Good man!" Again, he slapped Manny on the shoulder, and the other men shared in the amusement. Just then, a woman came through the door. It was the president who noted the sudden hesitancy in Manny's demeanor.

"Mr. Vallega, you seem surprised to see a woman joining us."

Manny eyed the woman with caution. Though he believed that most women were tools men used to get what they wanted, this one seemed to have deceit in her eyes.

"Not at all." Although Manny didn't like surprises, she was a pleasant looking one.

"Kate Frampton, Mr. Vallega. It's a pleasure to meet you."

Manny stood and shook her outstretched hand. "Ms. Frampton." Though he acknowledged her presence, he wasn't sure about the purpose of her appearance.

"The senators and the president thought we should discuss how my company might be beneficial to your cause. I see an explanation is in order. I am the president and CEO of ADDEX Pharmaceutical."

Manny felt the men studying his reaction, so he maintained an indifferent posture. "I think there has been some mistake, Ms. Frampton. My interest is in politics, not pharmaceuticals."

Ms. Frampton took a few steps back and leaned against the arm of Senator Bushman's chair. Though it was covered by her skirt, he took advantage of the situation and craned his neck for a better view of her ass.

"I can assure you, Mr. Vallega, you won't find anyone more accommodating in the corporate world than we are. We have a high rate of success in helping great men to find their place in political history. Wouldn't you like to be one of them?"

At her request to meet privately, Manny followed Kate Frampton into the room next door. Leaving the group, he'd initially planned to meet agitated him. He took a seat on a large leather chair positioned against the wall. This allowed him a clear view of the door. He wanted no more surprises; one was enough.

Kate closed the door and leaned against the back of the thick, polished wood. "Mr. Vallega, I'm sure you're wondering how a pharmaceutical company can assist with political aspirations. First, I'd like to let you know that I speak on behalf of ADDEX Pharmaceutical. As a company, of course, we like to see good people in positions of power, especially in politics. That way when a new drug is developed that can help the population, we have already laid the groundwork to build a rapport with those who have influence. This makes it mutually beneficial for those in power who need our help, and our pursuits as well."

Manny eyed her with suspicion. He liked things to go as planned, and this meeting had not. His team was supposed to have investigated those who not only could help him to achieve his aspirations yet would be easy to manipulate. This woman and her company had never come up in any conversation. The last thing he expected was to see a five-foot-nothing woman with a massive set of balls. She sure as hell was hiding them well under her skin-tight skirt.

"Ms. Frampton, I'm not quite sure why we're even here, much less what a pharmaceutical company has to do with it. I was meeting with gentlemen who have experience in the political arena. Our meeting was set because I rely on their honesty and expertise to help me achieve my goals for the benefit of my country. I have no interest in pharmaceuticals."

"Mr. Vallega—Manny. May I call you Manny?" She took a few steps toward him, hips swaying, arms crossed against her chest. "Manny, if you believe that all it takes it's a good man with good intentions to be the president of a country then you're a fool—and you don't know anything about politics."

The back of Manny's neck prickled with agitation. "Is it so much to ask that a politician could be honest and want to do an honest job for his people?"

The corner of his mouth cocked into a lopsided grin. He was well aware, that in this day and age, his comment was near ridiculous. Of course, he wouldn't let her know that. Kate smiled at him.

"Well, bless your heart, Mr. Vallega. I do believe that your intentions are honorable and that you want to do what is best for your people, but we at ADDEX know it's going to take more than good intentions for you to be elected so you can reach your goals." She grabbed a chair identical to the one Manny was sitting in and dragged it by the arm until it rested in front of him, then took a seat. Looking Manny in the eye, she gave him a pleasant smile. Her white blouse was open at the top, one more button than necessary, giving Manny a view of her porcelain skin. Her face was as flawless as her figure with only a hint of pink on her cheeks. Long, blonde hair hung over her shoulders in soft waves. Her eyes were crystal blue, the color striking against the black-rimmed glasses resting on a delicate nose. The skirt that he'd noted earlier had hiked up a few inches as she crossed slender legs. She was the exact opposite of his wife. She leaned in, giving Manny a better opportunity to view the swell of her breasts.

"Mr. Vallega, I'm going to be perfectly frank. Colombia has a drug problem—but then most countries do. The United States falls in that group. Although ADDEX Pharmaceutical is located in the US, our business is global. We are the exclusive manufacturer of a life-saving product. One that is administered when some unfortunate soul overdoses. Having the exclusivity in this area has gained us an honorable reputation and a healthy return on investment. This drug has not only saved thousands of lives but helped save families and businesses. I don't need to tell you that not all drug addicts are curled up in the corner of a dirty street. You and I both know that a person with a drug problem could be your banker, lawyer, or priest. I'm sure that, because of your wife's former profession, you know that drug abuse is fairly common in the fashion industry."

The woman was getting close to revealing some truth from his private life. Did she know that his cartel was the main supplier of cocaine to the fashion industry? If so, she was raising his suspicions that ulterior motives might be at play. If some United States politicians were able to nab the head of a drug cartel, it would boost their numbers from their constituents. "I'm sorry, Ms. Frampton. We're getting way off the topic of politics, and I'm not following. What does all of this have to do with me?"

A smile played at her lips as she leaned back in her chair. "We're prepared to make a sizable donation to your campaign. We want to see good people in positions of authority. Isn't that enough, Mr. Villega?"

"We're done here, Ms. Frampton. As much as I appreciate the offer, this conversation is going nowhere." They stared at each other for a few moments, then Manny stood. "It was nice meeting you, Ms. Frampton." He started toward the door, but Kate wasn't finished.

"If I were you, Manny, I wouldn't leave this room until you hear what I came here to say."

He stopped and turned toward her. Kate's expression had changed to one harsher than the one with which she'd initiated their conversation. "Have you ever heard the expression about one hand washing the other?" He nodded. "ADDEX is prepared to make a sizeable donation to your election campaign. We're hopeful it will assist you at the polls."

"And why would your company want to do that for me? Until ten minutes ago I wasn't even aware of its existence."

"We're hopeful you'll be elected. It's as simple as that. We like backing winners."

Though she had Manny's attention, he noted his surroundings. The door was still closed, but he wondered if there wasn't some type of listening device that has been placed in the office. This could be a trap. Kate noted his body language and let out a sigh. Standing from her seat, she approached him and spoke in a calm, quiet tone.

"Here's the bottom line, Manny, we are well aware of your business—and I'm not talking about real estate. I'm talking about the business you don't want anyone to know about. We've been watching you for several years, ever since the death of your predecessor. You're a talented man. You slide under the radar of law enforcement and the DEA, and have done so for a few years. The man who used to hold your position wasn't quite as professional as you are. He never aspired to be anything more than what he was—and we both know that.

"This is a mutually beneficial proposition, Manny. Our money will ensure a successful bid for the presidency, and, when you do win, you can help us. The heroin and opioid epidemics affect everyone—the United States, Colombia, and many other places. This is where we can be of assistance. The drug I spoke of earlier is costly, and there is much debate about its benefits. When you're in office, we're certain you'll see the importance of our product and will support our efforts."

Manny's eyes narrowed. "I know what you're trying to do and say. I assure you, people with bigger balls than you have tried to make that connection and failed."

"You're wrong. That isn't my intent. All I'm trying to say is that I admire you and what you've accomplished. You're an intelligent man—and cautious. By the way you've been eyeing this room, I'm sure that you think we have it bugged. I assure you that's not the case. The facts are that a drug problem has been created, and we have a solution. Who creates the problem is not our worry. We simply want to do business." She gave him a knowing smile. "Now. Do you understand what ADDEX and I are offering?"

Though it would require further investigation on his part, he liked where this was going. He nodded, and Kate held out her hand for a shake.

"You and ADDEX will benefit each other, Mr. Vallega. I'm sure of it."

Manny returned the handshake, eager to get out of the building and dig through the dirt of Kate's company. As he loosened his hold of her, she surprised him and held fast.

"Now, before we part," she said with a wide smile, "please know that ADDEX would like to gift the expectant parents. We know you have been waiting patiently for this child. We'd like to help."

Chapter 8

Manny

For the second time in as many days, Manny was on a plane. He'd left Washington D.C. with a slightly bitter taste in his mouth, somewhat irritated that he'd been duped. He needed the time on the plane to mull over all that had transpired.

He wasn't one for surprises. He chided himself for not being better prepared. He should have expected that when he got into bed with American politicians there would always be duplicity.

Kate Frampton and all she represented was unexpected. It would take some time to check out her story. If everything she said was right, it would take little effort on his part to put a plan in motion. In the short time he'd been in the air, Manny had educated himself about her company and their research and success with the drug she'd told him about.

Although he'd would never admit to having anything to do with its production, Colombia was responsible for most of the world's drug problems. Cocaine and heroin thinned out the herd, so to speak. The weak overdosed and died. If ADDEX was successful in reversing overdose situations, those same people would live long enough to purchase more drugs and possibly overdose another few times until they finally got it right. The truth was that Manny couldn't care less about the deaths. If he allowed Kate Frampton and ADDEX access to his world, he could keep his hands clean while filling them with cash.

The whole idea had merit. It could be entirely possible to reach the presidency and have no worries or suspicions by his public. ADDEX Pharmaceuticals was a reputable company and their donations wouldn't raise suspicions. Many major corporations made campaign contributions. In small enough amounts they raised no red flags while providing a nice tax write off for their respective companies. Their power wasn't only in dollars, and this was the part that interested Manny the most, their board members had their own little cliques. It was better to operate within small audiences of influence. His and Marianna's social circle would be increased with even more monied, powerful people. That was what Manny was after. The razor's edge that would allow him to travel simultaneously down the road of legal and illegal activity. ADDEX would pave those roads without him lifting a finger.

A flight attendant appeared and interrupted his thoughts. "Sr. Vallega, we'll be landing in about an hour. We alerted your driver, and upon doing so, we're told that your wife has been trying to reach you."

Manny peered over the side of his seat and into his briefcase. He had silenced his phone and thrown it down into the bag so that he could investigate ADDEX uninterrupted. Marianna rarely called him, and then only if there was a problem.

"Thank you."

As the attendant returned to the back of the plane, Manny retrieved his phone and pressed the number assigned to Marianna on speed dial.

"May I help you?" The voice belonged not to his wife, but to Teresa.

"Where is Sra. Vallega?" Marianna rarely had her phone out of her sight. The fact that Teresa answered alarmed him. Though he employed the ablest men to secure his home, there was always the chance that something could go wrong.

"The baby is coming."

The news was unexpected. The baby wasn't due to arrive for another few weeks. "Let me speak with her."

A few minutes and various muffled sounds later, which he could only guess were caused by the transfer of the phone, he heard his wife's voice.

"Hello?" Marianna's tone was strained.

"Marianna? Tell me what's happening."

"The baby will be here. Soon."

He leaned forward in his seat and wiped a hand over his face. This wasn't how this was supposed to go. He was supposed to be there with Marianna when the baby arrived. He didn't want her assistant to be the first person to see it. A child should be greeted by its mother and father before presented to anyone else. He hit the mute button on the phone and shouted toward the cockpit. "How long until we land?"

"One hour, thirteen minutes until we're on the tarmac, Sir."

He unmuted the phone. "I'll be there in an hour and a half, Marianna. Wait for my arrival."

Chapter 9

A ria

I FOLLOWED the ray of light with my eyes. It peeked through the cracks and slivers of space that remained through the closed blinds. I didn't have the energy to move. How long had I been lying here? An hour? A day? Several? I didn't know or care. All I cared about was my daughter, and she was gone.

"Aria."

I recognized my mother's voice, but I didn't want to move. If I did, I was sure I would lose what was left of my sanity. Exhausted from crying, my emotions were chained to the bed. I held on to Karas's blanket, inhaling her scent with closed eyes. So many unanswered questions whipped my mind with the lash of introspection. I was so numb I barely felt my mother's hand.

"Aria, you have to get up."

Ignoring her, I closed my eyes in response. I didn't want to see or talk to anyone. My daughter had been gone for months, and in that time her kidnapping had gone from a national news story to a blip during the evening telecast. Even the police told us we had to hope for the best but prepare ourselves for the worst. I crucified myself every day with the reality of her disappearance, driving nails through my heart as I remembered every tiny detail about my little girl. Her laugh. Her smile. Her eyes. I was terrified that if I didn't commit them to memory every day, she would be gone from me forever. My mother came around to my side of the bed. My eyes were closed, and I felt the bed dip beneath her weight and caught the mild scent of her perfume.

"I know this is hard. I know you want to crawl into a hole, but I'm not going to let you do that."

I didn't move. I didn't even look at my mother to acknowledge her presence. She placed a gentle hand on my back and moved her fingers in tiny circles.

"Sweet girl, we've been down this road before, remember? You're stronger than this, Aria. You have to fight. You have to fight it, or there's no hope for Karas."

An air of indignation filled my lungs. "What more

can I do? If the police and the FBI have no leads, what makes you think that I can do anything?" I rolled away from my mother, turning onto the opposite side to escape the recrimination I felt. I wanted my mom to leave, but she laid down behind me, her arm closing around my waist. For a fraction of a moment, I felt comfort, just like when I was a little girl. Immediately after that, I tensed. If my baby couldn't feel the pleasure of a mother's touch, then I had no right to enjoy it either. My mother tightened her hold.

"I want you to listen to me." Her tone was soft but firm. "No one loves your daughter more than you. She is the only one who knows the intimacy of your heartbeat. You are a strong woman—stronger than you know. Against all the odds you carried her and gave her to all of us. Even your husband doesn't know that baby as well as you do. You fought back depression once; you can do it again. You and Karas share an unbreakable tether. You need to muster your strength. That little girl is going to need you when she comes home."

Uninvited, the tears began to flow. My body betrayed me on a daily, if not hourly, basis. One minute I felt strong and determined, the next weak and defeated.

"You've lost weight." My mother's comment was delivered with a heavy dose of concern. I felt the bed move again, and then she gripped my arm. "C'mon. It's time to get up."

I resisted, pulling my arm back against her tug, but she persisted. I wanted to fight her; I wanted to press myself into the soft linen sheets until I disappeared, but my mom was stronger. As she pulled, my body slid to the side of the bed.

"Mom, stop!" She ignored my protest and continued until I nearly fell off the edge. I put my leg down in a contorted twist to keep from hitting the floor and awkwardly stood.

"There now. That's the first step."

My mother could be quite the little bulldog when the need arose. Though she was tiny in stature, she had a fierce determination about her. Up until now, I'd thought I was just like her. I turned to face her, looking down into her eyes. "I can't do this, Mom."

"Yes, you can."

The confidence in her expression humbled me. My mom had weathered more storms in the form of life events than one person should ever bear, yet here she stood, ready to fight another battle.

"Do you think my heart isn't broken? You're my daughter. She's my granddaughter. If ever there was a time you needed to pull yourself together, it's now. Karas doesn't have a chance without you, Aria. You are the one who needs to make calls every day, follow every lead, remind the police and anyone who will listen there's a little girl who needs to be found. A sweet baby who needs her mother. You need to remind Declan to use his contacts. You have to show your face at the police station. You have to say the name of your daughter to everyone who will listen—and as many times as you have a voice. You need to make them sick of seeing you because of your persistence. You will find her." I tried to look away, but she wouldn't have it. She wrapped her hands around the top of each of my arms. "You will find her," she emphasized. "There is no other option."

I'm not sure what happened at that moment. I don't know if it was the determination in my mom's eyes, in her voice, or a combination of both, but I felt this weird infusion of strength as I looked at her. Her hold on me connected us, and her energy flowed through me as if an intravenous line of hope and purpose had opened and flooded my veins. A surge of ambition and tenacity electrified the dormant synapsis rousing them from their comatose state. My mother's blue eyes sparkled with fiery silver sparks. Like bullets, they fired through me, leaving bits of shrapnel, pieces of determination, but doubt still had a hold on my heart.

"But, Mom—"

"No buts, Aria. No doubts. No questions. I don't want you to think of anything other than Karas. You are her mother. Her defender. Her warrior."

"But what if she's—"

Again, she interrupted. "Do you feel her? That's all you have to ask yourself. Do you feel her?"

I closed my eyes, searching for an answer. For the

first time in weeks, I passed through my own anxious thoughts and centered myself. I focused on my daughter. My girl. My baby. Karas. I knew the answer all the way to my core.

"Yes."

Chapter 10

Aria

My mother was right. About everything. I had lost weight. I couldn't let my emotions drag me down. My daughter needed me. I was determined to get her back.

As I stood in the shower, conviction washed over me. I hugged myself beneath the soaking spray of water. With soapy hands, my fingers trailed slowly over my skin. The difference over just a few months was visible. My ribs poked against my flesh and were more prominent, as were my hip bones. My skin was dry and cracked and thirsted for moisture. I had completely let myself go since the moment Karas had disappeared. I tried to recall details of the event, this time more rationally and without hysteria. The twin bitches of sadness and depression still had me in their grip, but I fought them. I'd allowed grief to live rent-free inside of me for far too long. I knew in my heart Karas was alive. My daughter deserved no less than my best fight.

I hated revisiting the day she was taken, but I had to remember every moment if I was to find her. Somewhere in the dark recesses of my mind was a clue. Somewhere there was an answer. *Somewhere Karas is crying for me.* I had to find her.

Closing my eyes, I let the hot water beat on my sore neck and shoulder muscles. With eyes tightly closed I allowed the events of November eleventh to play through my mind. Like an old-time movie, I staggered each frame in my mind's eye as I looked for anything that might be significant.

It was a warm day, especially since the summer season had ended. The melody in the air wasn't the music from the Ferris Wheel or the Matterhorn, it was Karas's sweet giggle.

It was conjured by playing with a mobile, its sound mixed with the crash of ocean waves on the shore. Decorated with round discs painted to look like the faces of the sloths, it was attached to the cloth covered bar on the front of her stroller. She had a thing for the slow-moving animals when she saw them on an Animal Planet television show. After that whenever she spied anything sloth related her eyes would light up with excitement, her bottom bouncing in concert with outstretched hands that itched to get ahold of the item. Her vocabulary was not yet developed. "Da-da," "Ma-

ma," and "Ba-ba" were favorites, but she babbled in a language known only to her most of the time.

As I walked down the boardwalk, Karas batted the mobile. It had jingling bells inside, and I gauged her activity according to the tinkling sound; more sound meant she was wide awake, where none indicated she'd fallen asleep.

We walked nearly every day, well into late fall or early winter. I'd pull the top down, snapping it closed to protect her tender skin from the cold, salt air. She was a mama's girl, always checking through the transparent window at the top to make sure I was still there.

Karas was bright-eyed and energetic that day, while I was the exact opposite. I hadn't slept well the night before, and rain was predicted later that day. I needed caffeine to fuel me. The further I pushed the stroller the more dragged out I felt. In retrospect, I wished I'd never gone outside at all. If only I'd skipped a day.

The aroma of freshly roasted coffee beans enticed me. It floated in the air, a fragrance I couldn't resist. I looked around, anxious to get my fix. After scanning the storefronts, a pinkish, neon "Open" sign beckoned to me. I turned the stroller and headed in the direction of a new place, "The Grinding Halt." It was kind of cute, quaint even. It was across the street from a church with doors painted barn red. Like many little shops, you had a choice of either stepping inside or placing an order at a counter on the outside, which I guessed was open because it was a sunny day. I stepped up to the counter *where a guy who looked to be in his early twenties greeted me.*

"Yes, ma'am."

Ma'am? Although I was older than him, I wasn't old. I rolled my eyes at him. "Really?"

"Hey, my mom raised me right!" he laughed. "What can I get you?"

"Coffee, sweet and light, with a shot of espresso. The largest you've got."

"Coming right up."

I was wearing a backpack and slid my arms out of the straps to get cash. I sat it on top of the counter to get out my wallet, turning the stroller to the side and anchoring it with my foot.

While Karas watched scores of workmen as they traveled down the street, one or two waved at her. Seagulls screeched nearby hoping to get some bites of French fries or funnel cakes.

"Looks busy around here today," I called to the young man waiting on me.

"Yeah, it's been crazy all morning. This is the first time it's slowed down. Those guys bring their thermoses and get me to fill them up. I think I've made fifty pots today."

Although confident his count of fifty pots was an exaggeration, I humored him. I paid little attention as he got my order, leaning my wallet on the edge of the counter. When I looked up, he was smiling.

"Three fifty, and I didn't put your sweetener in. I figured you'd want to do that yourself."

Again, I nodded and fished for a five dollar bill. Just as I was about to pull it out a man beside me plunked his thermos on the counter and BAAM! The hot coffee tipped over, spilling inside my jacket, and soaking my tee shirt.

"Ow!" I jumped back, the contents of my backpack and wallet spilling all over the ground.

"Oh my God! Sorry, lady!"

Both men yanked napkins from the holder and practically threw them at me and, as I dabbed at my chest, I dropped to the ground to grab the money. The older man tried to pick up lipstick, a compact mirror, and a pacifier, while the younger man came out the door of the shop and helped me retrieve the cash and contents of my wallet. It was pandemonium for a time.

As they shoved handfuls of everything at me, I dumped them in the backpack. I could sort everything at home, where I could get out of the damn, wet shirt.

"Thanks. Thank you. Thanks a lot." I repeated various versions of the phrase several times, not wanting to seem ungrateful. I grabbed at a few remaining items like I was playing with a ball and jacks, not looking at everything, just playing pick-up. The wind picked up, causing Karas's fuzzy, pink hat to blow by my foot. I snatched it. My foot had dislodged its hold on the stroller, and it was about a foot away. I stood up and grabbed the handle. As I bent over to put the hat back on her, my heart leaped into my throat. Where was she?

Fear.

Icy fingers around my throat.

Oxygen stolen by a death grip on my lungs.

Terror ripping away my voice.

"Lady?"

I looked but didn't see him. I held fast to the hat, fisting it. My fingernails clawing through the cabled knit. Blood droplets in my palms. He looked at me and then looked down, following my line of sight toward the sidewalk.

"Oh my God, lady! Where's your baby?"

Chapter 11

ria

I GRABBED a towel from the hook outside of the shower and wrapped it around my head. As I pressed out the moisture, I tried to clear my head. Because I blamed myself, I realized I was responsible for more than Karas's disappearance. I'd pushed away my husband and distanced myself from friends and family but, after my talk with my mom, I saw that if we all pulled together as a team, we had a better chance of finding her.

I continued drying my body, noting the escape of steam when the door opened slightly.

"Aria?" Declan appeared through the drift of

vapor. "Babe, when you're finished, I need to talk to you."

"What's wrong?"

"Nothing. We might have news."

I picked up the pace, slipping into yoga pants and a tee shirt and flipping my hair up into a messy bun. As I hurried down the hall, I saw Declan sitting at the end of our sofa. His expression was serious. I took a seat beside him.

"Tell me." My body trembled as I looked at my husband. As if I was seeing him for the first time, I noticed the dark circles around his eyes. Though the impact of our daughter's disappearance hit both of us differently, it was evident Declan had suffered as much as me. Pangs of shame and guilt hit my heart. I'd allowed him to walk this nightmare alone yet, as he looked at me, all I saw was love and concern in his eyes.

"Carter called. I just got off the phone with him." He took my hand in his.

"Another false sighting?"

Declan's brother, Carter, owned a security company and had a background in law enforcement. His contacts in those areas offered us more hope of finding our daughter than the newspapers and local police. He'd gotten the FBI involved and, together with his partners, had put eyes and ears out to the dark web to scout anything that would lead to Karas.

Declan had followed his brother's progress and was as proactive with the investigation as the different agencies would allow. I'd been just the opposite, preferring to wallow in my self-imposed prison. Upon learning the news, Carter and his wife, Aimee, had immediately came to our home. They'd stayed with us for three weeks. While Carter had investigated every lead, Aimee had done her best to console me. None of the leads had proven solid; many were false, and each one of those had ripped my heart apart and sent me deeper into depression. I was determined that no matter the news today, I would stay strong.

"He and Aimee are on their way back to the beach. He's come across another lead. It could be nothing, though, so—"

"Don't get my hopes up. I know," I interrupted.

"Yeah."

These days my emotions were a frequent rider on an unsecured seat of a roller-coaster. As I looked at my husband, guilt stabbed me in the heart. My self-absorption had left him to face all this alone. When he'd needed me most, I hadn't been there for him. He looked terrible. Not at all like the days when he was in front of the camera modeling. He was thinner. Lines that I hadn't noticed before etched his handsome face. Although we'd reacted very differently, the toll of losing our daughter had affected us both in similar ways.

He offered me a weak smile. "You look better today."

"I'm trying," I answered, responding with a tender smile of my own. He put his forehead to mine.

"That's all we can do, baby. We don't have much of a choice." He took my hand, caging it with his own. Fingers entwined and hearts now set on the same course, I felt connected in a way I'd nearly forgotten. I reached a hand to his face, tracing the lines of his jaw with my fingers. The feel of his whisker stubble abraded the tender skin at the tips, my fingernails long since bitten down. I'd missed him and the tender intimacy that came from enjoying each other's touch. I'd allowed numbing sorrow to consume me for far too long. That stopped today. Other than crying my heart out as Declan held me in his arms, I hadn't enjoyed my husband since my baby had been taken. I had convinced myself that, if my daughter couldn't enjoy her snuggles from family and friends, neither could I. It wasn't rational. It wasn't fair. It wasn't right thinking. The look on my husband's face convicted me. Silently, I promised myself that, no matter what, I would never shut him out again. Instead, I would be his lifeline, and he would be mine.

"I'm so sorry." The words came out like a quiet confession, much like I'd learned to do in my church when I was a little girl.

No words fell from his lips as he swallowed hard. A soft and tender look fell over his gaze, and he squeezed my hand. It was all the reconciliation we needed. We had more important things than hurt feelings on which to concentrate.

"Tell me everything that Carter said. Don't leave anything out."

He leaned back against the sofa. "He said that he needed to talk to us again, especially you."

"But I've told him everything I remember."

"I know. Carter said that something unexpected came to light. Something he wasn't looking for. It had to do with Falcon and Marcus. Apparently, there's another division of MarSin Falcon. Some type of special security service that deals with international work. I thought it had to do with foreign dignitaries, but I'm not sure. All I know is that something turned up during one of their details."

My heart thundered in my chest, while my stomach did somersaults. For sixty-one days, ten hours, and thirteen minutes there'd been a gaping hole in my heart. This was the first I felt hopeful. It was a positive gut feeling. Although cautiously optimistic, I felt energized with renewed hope after a month of barely leaving my bed.

It's funny how life changes things. You go about your everyday life, taking even the simplest things for granted. First, it's you and your husband making this little life for the two of you. You fall into a routine, and then a child enters the picture. Life changes in an instant. Everything that had become a priority now takes second place to the happiness and well-being of this sweet little creature that looks a bit like both of you. Though your baby is more work and worry than you thought possible, the trade-off is the happiness discovered in your love for them. Life as you knew it would never be the same, but it didn't matter because you forgot what life was like before they arrived. Love changes everything. That's how our lives had been from the moment we held Karas in our arms.

My mom came into the living room from the kitchen. "I made the two of you something to eat. Some chicken salad for lunch and a casserole for dinner. There should be plenty for Carter and Aimee as well. It's in the fridge."

My stomach did somersaults just thinking about food, and the flips weren't the good kind. Still, I appreciated Mom making something because cooking was the last thing on my mind.

Mom slipped her arms into her jacket and retrieved her purse from the blue chair beside the door. As she headed toward us, Declan and I stood. He was considerably taller than her. It always made me smile to see this hulk of a guy bend over so she could give him a kiss and a hug. It was comical and endearing. "Call me if you need anything." She bussed his cheek.

"Thanks, Jeannie. For everything."

As always, she poo-pooed his comment with a gentle wave of her hand and then she came over to me. As we embraced, I leaned into the comfort of my mother's arms a little more than I usually did. A pang of guilt punched my gut knowing that my sweet baby couldn't do the same.

"Eat." Her whispered command brushed against my ear. I inhaled the familiar scent of my mother's perfume. She always wore the same fragrance. Just inhaling a whiff of it settled my nerves a bit. She pulled back and placed her hand on my cheek. "Don't make me nag you, Aria, okay? You have to eat so that you can build up some strength to bring our girl home."

I nodded, tears stinging my eyes. "I can't promise, but I'll try."

She smiled at me. If a look could will strength into a person, my mother was doing that. I felt stronger than I had when she'd dragged me out of bed and could only hope I could concentrate on going forward, instead of looking back. Confidence showed in her eyes. It humbled me. "You're a fighter, Aria. You can do this. You don't have a choice."

Chapter 12

A ria

Declan and I sipped our coffee as we waited for Carter and Aimee to arrive. There wasn't much to say as we both silently speculated on what Carter and Aimee's visit would bring. An actual solid lead or false hope? We tortured ourselves in our own individual ways, but the comfort of leaning on each other would combine our strength and maybe—just maybe—at the end of this we could find our little girl.

"A penny for your thoughts." The rich timbre of Declan's voice wrapped around me like a warm blanket.

"I'm not sure you'd want to hear them."

"Try me."

As I looked into his eyes, I saw no conviction there. How loving a man was my husband that he refused to incriminate me for losing what was so precious to us both? Yet there was none. He'd never accused or blamed me. I fell into the love reflected in the chocolaty pools.

"You've never blamed me. I've been waiting every day for you to snap and lash out at me, but you haven't. I almost wish you would yell and scream and get it over with."

"Why would I do that? You're not to blame." His brows pinched together as his expression tensed the lines on his forehead.

"I don't know how you can say that." I looked away, not feeling worthy of his love. "It's all my fault, Declan. I was the one who insisted Karas get fresh air every day. As long as it wasn't pouring down rain, I'd put her in the stroller and take her for a long walk on the boardwalk. It was my selfishness. You know how I love being by the ocean, and being in the house every day with a baby can, sometimes, make you stir-crazy. I needed to get out. I wanted her to love being outside by the water as much as I did. I wanted it to be something that we would share as she grew up. I could picture us having mother/daughter chats about boys and clothes. I even pictured us getting fries to feed the damn seagulls, and now . . ."

My voice trailed off as the images in my mind's eye became almost too painful to bear. Karas's chubby fingers opening and closing as the birds came close. She looked like she was trying to pluck them out of the sky for playmates. The expression of wonderment on her sweet face was before me. Her crystal clear, blue eyes watering in sunlight as she looked up at the clouds. I clung to the sound of her laugh as my lifeline, terrified I'd never again hear the lilt in her voice. That it would fade away, and I would have to struggle to remember it, in much the same way as I did my father's.

"And now we do whatever we have to, so we get through this, and bring her home." He tightened his arm around me. "I don't feel that she's gone, do you? I think she's still alive. I know the police said that the more time that passes, the less chance we have of getting her back, but I think they're wrong. I think she's alive, and I have to believe we'll find her."

My eyes stung as fresh tears surfaced. Karas was alive, I knew it in my gut. There was a tether between us and whenever I began to lose hope, her laugh would tickle my ears. Oh, God, please bring our baby home!

I turned, looking up into my husband's weary eyes. He cupped my cheeks, his thumbs wiping away my tears while his own fell.

"So much has been stolen from us. She was on the verge of her first steps. Maybe she's even strung together a few words. She's so damned independent! I'll bet she misses us as much as we miss her."

"I know she does." I could only whisper, but I offered the words of comfort. Declan hadn't asked for one thing through all of this, but now I could see he was as tortured as I was.

I held him, and he held me. He reached for a picture of Karas from the side table. Her nose was wrinkled, her grin bearing two bottom teeth, and her eyes scrunched as she looked up at a blue sky. Her hands were full of wet sand, and her expression was due to the new adventure of holding it. Like a fist, the memory of that day punched at both of us.

"We have to get her back, Aria. We just have to."

I held him as he rested his head on my shoulder. He traced the lines of the photo with his thumb, caressing Karas's image. I stroked his hair as, for the first time, he shucked the strong veneer and allowed the sorrow to flow.

After a few minutes, he looked at me. His red-rimmed eyes framed unmistakable exhaustion. Now it was my turn to will determination and strength to him.

"It's exactly as you said, my love. We'll get her back."

Chapter 13

I had always had a soft spot for cats and, as much as I didn't want to admit it, this baby's cry reminded me of a kitten. Still, I kept my distance.

"Teresa, how is the girl doing today?"

"She's good. Please. Come see."

I went closer to the scene. Teresa and the baby were sitting on the floor playing pat-a-cake. Nonsense, really, but I had to admit the child was cute.

"Come sit with us, señora. Play."

Teresa smiled at me. I rolled my eyes, but I knew a smile teased my lips. The idea of me, in designer clothes, sitting on the floor, playing a child's game? Ludicrous. But then, I had to get used to her. She was my daughter and, despite my worry as to whether I would like her looks, she was cute.

This wasn't what I'd expected, but I had little to complain about. Manny had proposed the idea by appealing to my like of both clothes and decorating. When I'd resisted, saying I liked the nightlife and entertainment, he'd assured me the child would always be secondary and that our social life would remain a priority. I'd accepted, believing I'd make everything beautiful and ready for the baby's arrival and that Teresa would care for it. Manny had the connections and took care of all the details. My few months away from the public eye was to bond with our adopted child. After that time, I'd return to Manny's side to attend functions and plan parties. It was a perfect plan. *Except you like this kid.*

I pushed away from the thought. Even when I had a kitten, I had someone else clean the litter box. I only did the things I liked with it. I held it, petted it, and put pretty stuff on it. *Just like the baby.*

The internal monologue hadn't ceased. I didn't want to like the girl, but I did. Silently I harbored a fear I could lose this Eliana just as I had my childhood friend. *But you had no control over that situation. You have all the power now.*

I stood tall, proud at that thought. Yes! I did have control. I was no longer a child, and my father no longer held all the cards. My husband had endured much the same as I had when we were growing up, but we survived. He was now in control of the cartel, and I was in control of my destiny. I would be the first lady of Colombia, and I could do what I wanted with this baby. My first step was in asserting myself as her mother. Manny had initially been the one to choose Eliana's nanny, and I'd fired her.

It wasn't pretty. It had been a showdown. I'd told the nanny her services were no longer needed. As expected, she'd informed Manny. He was incensed that I would usurp his authority, but I held my ground. He argued that Teresa was too old. That she couldn't correctly see to my needs and that of a baby as well. I held firm to my conviction. Teresa wasn't old, she was sixty, and she'd helped me through many things. Though I hadn't appreciated her at the time, I trusted Teresa with my life and appealed to his obsessive need for privacy.

Teresa had proven her loyalty to me over the years, and I knew she'd help both Eliana and I to adjust, no matter how easy or difficult the process of our bonding would be. I'd schooled him on the press and how hungry they'd be for any negative news story. I'd told him I refused to chance that anything would be said about him and I and our parenting. Having Teresa with Eliana and me would eliminate any negative light casting a shadow on our public persona. She'd help me to be the best mother possible. He'd agreed, though reluctantly. I'd won; Eliana was mine.

I looked down at the two of them playing. The nursery was filled with happy giggles and sweet smiles. The baby had only been with us a few months, and I was cautiously getting closer to her. *Liar!*

The conviction came hard and swift. If I was ever

going to go public as a mother, I needed to bond with this child. Though the title of "mami" fit me like an itchy sweater, it was one I now wore. There was no going back. Manny was . . . well, Manny. But Eliana . . . Eliana was mine. Shaping her into a little Marianna might be fun.

I feared raising this child was going to destroy my social life. Nonetheless, we'd both agreed it would be beneficial all the way around to add a child to our home. Our advantage was that, to the public, we would look like a loving family, and the child would benefit from having its material needs met.

There was no room for shying away from my role. Manny wouldn't hear of it. But he was the product of a patriarchal society. One where men did business and women cared for babies. He thought Eliana was cute, but he saw her as a nonperson. He said that no one would notice a father being a bit distant, but it was unacceptable for a mother to be that way. At first, I resented that way of thinking, but then I realized that Eliana and I had one thing in common; we were both pawns in a game of political chess.

She was just as much a victim as I was in that regard, but since her care and adjustment were left solely to me and Teresa, I could use that to unite us. I could teach Eliana to be just like me, and, when she was grown, perhaps we could get Manny out of the way and mother and daughter would co-rule the cartel. The thought had a delicious appeal.

I savored the idea as I took a seat in the rocking chair. Teresa and Eliana were still clapping hands with the pat-a-cake game while I watched. Eliana crawled to Teresa. She gripped tiny fistfuls of the blouse sleeve covering Teresa's arm and pulled herself up. She cocked her head and began to babble excitedly. Apparently, she was proud of her accomplishment.

She then turned to me, her gaze going over my shoulder and turning severe.

"You are a study in maternal bliss, my dear."

Manny's voice made me cringe internally. I maintained my composure, never letting on that I hated him trespassing in the nursery.

"She's a beautiful child. We're lucky to have her."

Eliana didn't make a sound. I watched her as she watched Manny. I'd always heard that children have a sixth sense. If that were true, the expression on her face said she didn't trust him. Yet another thing we had in common.

"I want Teresa to take a few pictures."

"Why?"

"New fathers brag about their children. God knows I've had to suffer through enough family pictures at meetings and parties. It wouldn't look good if I didn't have pictures of my own family." He tipped his chin at Teresa. "Stand her over there, by the pink hassock."

Teresa did as instructed but stayed by Eliana's side so that she wouldn't fall.

"Move out of the way, Teresa."

She obeyed his order, but the moment she left Eliana, she began to pout.

"C'mon, girl. Smile for your papi."

Manny held the phone up, ready to take the shot, and Eliana started to cry.

"Oh, for God's sake! Shut her up."

Teresa started to go to the baby, but he stopped her. "Not you." He looked at me. "You."

"What?" I gave him an incredulous look. "Nonsense," I said turning away from him. "Teresa, you can get her."

"I said no, Marianna. You get her."

Eliana's wails increased in intensity. I looked from the baby to him. "What is your problem?"

"My problem is that I have no pictures of mother and child. You've told me she's adjusting. Now show me."

There was an edginess in his voice that unnerved me, and it seemed to have the same effect on the baby.

"Fine!" I walked over to Eliana. She was holding on to the ottoman, looking lost and afraid. A fist of emotion squeezed my heart. She didn't like Manny controlling things any more than I did. I reached for her, slipping my hands under the crook of her arms. "Come here, *chica*." She responded by leaning into my hold. Raising her up, I placed her on my hip. I ignored Manny, speaking directly to Eliana. "No need to fear. Mami's got you."

"Ma-ma-ma-ma-ma." Eliana's mouth popped open and closed, her lips curved inward to form the pronounced "M." I smiled at her. In her own little way, she let me know she didn't like the mean man any more than I did. I turned to Manny.

"Take your picture."

Chapter 14

A ria

CARTER DIDN'T KNOCK; he quietly entered with Aimee right behind him.

"Hey, brother." As Carter and Declan embraced in that all-too-familiar, testosterone filled "I love you, man" slap on the back, I greeted Aimee. Carter's veneer was the very definition of tense. I could nearly feel it permeate the air. As I stepped away from Aimee, I could see that she, too, wore a severe expression. We went into the living room. Aimee and I took a seat on the sofa while our husbands each took a chair. Carter looked to Aimee, who gave him a nod and a weak smile.

"I'm just going to start because I do have news. For

it to make sense, I have to start at the beginning." He sat back in the chair and crossed a leg, resting his ankle on his knee. "We have expanded MarSin Falcon. We now have a global division to deal with international accounts. It started as just one job, and Marcus was handling that end of it. The result was so successful that it grew quickly. Within a few months, actually. Now, it's the major source of revenue for the company. Some are big assignments, some are small, but all are equally important, at least, to us they are. Occasionally Falcon joins him. It all depends on the particulars and, for many of the jobs, there is a confidentiality clause because the clients can be politicians, international dignitaries, judges—you get the idea. Although most pose no national threats and the papers get some of the details, other missions are strictly covert. We haven't made this part of the company very visible. No advertising. Strictly word of mouth. Most of the contracts have been procured through highly classified, government agencies."

He paused, looking at us both until he was satisfied we were following, and then continued. "The good thing is that, because we do work these covert missions, the technology we have at our disposal is the latest, greatest, and most invasive that's made. We can hear what people are saying and see what they're doing. I'm not just talking Google Earth here, I'm talking about all that stuff that Edward Snowden revealed about listening in, and watching us, on cell phones and computers. And that isn't all. There's more advanced stuff that they give us access to. It has to do with surveillance on the dark web and accessing NSA databases. The riskier and more dangerous a situation appears, the more access they give us to ensure a successful mission."

I looked from Carter to Declan, unable to imagine what our situation had to do with the dark web. My husband's expression was grave.

"What does any of this have to do with my daughter? You're talking spy shit in the same breath that you're talking about my little girl." Declan's tone was thick with agitation.

"I'm getting to that," Carter said. "Give me a minute!" His tone was abrasive, defensive almost. It earned stern looks from us all, but Aimee shot him a hard look.

"Please stop. Now is not the time to have a big boy pissing contest. Focus on the matter at hand." Carter let out a sigh in response, but I noted a slight tip of his chin as he looked at her. An acknowledgment of an unspoken message she'd relayed through her gaze.

He shifted his attention to Declan. "Look, I don't mean to be insensitive. I'm just hoping that what we've seen, and what I have to tell you, will have some merit." Carter took a moment, inhaled a deep breath, and closed his eyes. For a moment, he appeared to be centering himself as one would do in yoga. When, a moment later, he opened them, his countenance had changed. Gone was the buzzing, high energy tone with which he had been speaking. It was replaced with a calmer, gentler tone of voice.

"There's so much intel we have to sift through to be certain, but Karas is my niece and goddaughter. I love her almost as much as you do." He once again looked at Aimee. "We don't know if kids are in the picture for us. She's the closest we may come to it.

"I debated whether or not I should let you in on all of this because we don't have anything concrete yet, but if it were my girl, I'd want to know everything."

I struggled to swallow the lump in my throat. My mouth was parched, having gone dry the minute Carter began to talk about dark webs and covert operations in the same sentences as my daughter's name. Panic began its ascent from low in my belly, inching its way up to my heart. As I took in Declan's body language, it appeared he was ready for a fight.

"Just cut to the chase. Tell us what you know," he urged Carter.

"Ok, but keep in mind that all of this is speculation at this point, okay?"

Declan nodded at his brother, and Carter continued. "Some foreign elections will be taking place this year. Our global division I was telling you about has been contracted to guard the sitting president of Argentina. There has been some unrest, and his supporters are fearful that an attempt on his life is imminent. Most of the operations involving him have felt more like babysitting. They're uneventful. Lots of parties and cocktail receptions where we keep an eye on him and his wife. I don't have to tell you that all these politicians are ass-kissers. They wine and dine each other, all while trying to get their supporters, backers, and interested companies to empty their pockets into the campaign funds. Of course, we couldn't give two shits about who washes whose back. Our mission was simple; keep the president safe and alive.

"Two weeks ago Marcus contacted me to tell me there was a big charity event on the schedule and that the president and his wife were the big names on the ticket. The event was supposed to draw one thousand supporters, both of the charity and the president. His attendance meant he was the draw for the charity.

"Initially, we'd only scheduled a team of three to watch over them, but Marcus felt more eyes and guns were needed. If I didn't send more people over, it could be a recipe for disaster because we wouldn't have enough manpower to do our job. Falcon and I decided he should go and take another two guys. Marc and Fal have a good feel for what they do, and they've worked together before, so they know just what's needed to have each other's backs.

"As it turned out, Marc had been rotating his crew of three until sleep was a little threadbare. Falcon had a few guys that filled the exact positions that Marc's team did, so they were able to plant two men on each post. One of the guys is a computer whiz. Falcon put him behind the screen the moment his boots hit the ground. Fresh eyes. That's where your situation comes into play."

Carter leaned over the side of the chair and pulled a file out of his backpack. He opened it up and handed a piece of paper to Declan and me. "Take a look at this for a minute."

I took the paper in my hand, but I didn't scrutinize it. I was done with the cloak and dagger conversation, and I couldn't imagine what connection there could be between the president of Argentina, a security force, and a baby, and I didn't want to try and figure it out. I itched for Carter to just tell us what all of this had to do with Karas.

"What do you make of this? Anything?" he asked.

I studied it for a few minutes, but the more I looked at it, the more I didn't see. Declan, however, seemed to be focused on something in particular.

"These two. They look familiar," Declan said, pointing at two people.

"Because they are. His back is to you, but you can see the side of her face."

Declan's face went pale, and then he looked up at his brother. "Marisol."

The name escaped him like he'd been sucker punched, while I, sitting on the edge of my seat, nearly toppled forward.

"Oh my God, Carter." My voice went up an octave

with a shrill cry. "What are you saying? That Marisol and Manny have our baby?"

"We don't know," he said, shaking his head. "All we have to go on is a piece of a conversation picked up on a listening device. It seems that the president congratulated Manny and Marisol on their new daughter. I didn't know she was pregnant. Did you?"

Chapter 15

A ria

We concluded that there was no way Marisol could have been pregnant and not make the news. Even if it was only one tiny article in *People*, it would have been noted. Carter, Falcon, and Marcus were given a giant clue, and we asked them to play detective.

As Carter's office wanted to get on this as soon as possible, Declan offered the use of his office at his business, The Studio, so he could touch base with Falcon and Marcus for updates. Whereas Carter's assistance to us initially had been pro bono, we refused his generosity this time. We signed on the dotted line, contracting the company formally to use whatever means necessary to find

Karas. There were no limits to what we would do to find out any information that could lead to her return.

Aimee, although tired from the nearly six-hour drive, offered to take us out for lunch. Having lost our appetite once the name Marisol was mentioned, there was no way we could eat.

Once Declan had carried her overnight bag up to the guestroom, Aimee excused herself saying she was going to shower and change. When he came down the steps, I followed him into the kitchen.

His shoulders were slumped as he silently walked over to the window. It was a beautiful day, one we would have enjoyed if we weren't in the middle of a chaotic quagmire. Our hands were tied. We couldn't even go to the police or press because we had no concrete evidence.

He stared outside, his blank look tearing at my heart. I could do nothing to help him as the hole inside of me grew both wide and deep. The peaceful landscape of blue sky and sandy beach offering neither one of us the solace we so desperately needed. As I looked at him, I could see his eyes were on one thing, but his mind was on another.

How many questions have no answers? How far could we bend before we broke? I didn't have a clue. If we were to be effective in bringing our baby home, no matter where she was, we had to concentrate, get our heads on straight, dig deep, and search for the positives.

Find the light in a dark situation. All we had to rely on was each other and hope.

I stretched far and reached deep down for the positives within the negatives. *If* Marisol had the baby at least that meant she was alive.

Patiently, I waited for Declan to say something, but as time passed by it was evident he had no words. I went to him, my fingertips slightly grazing the top of his forearm. He didn't even notice.

"Hey." He turned toward me, his eyes red-rimmed and brimming with tears. I died a little seeing the turmoil etched in his face. "Tell me what's going through your head. I'm trying to see the bright side of this news. Karas . . . we can get her back if this pans out. Unless there's something you're not telling me."

"Don't you see, Aria? If what Carter suspects is true, then it's my fault. If it weren't for me, Karas wouldn't be missing."

"How can you say that? That's not true. I was the one who turned away from her at that damn coffee shop. I should never have gone out that morning."

"You only did what any normal person would do if their money were all over the ground. It's me. Me and my history with Marisol. I'm the one that put you and our daughter at risk. It's all on me; Lacey's death, my brother's grief, your breakdown, Aimee's rape, Paige . . . all of it. Hell, even getting hit by the car was my own damned fault. I should have just kicked her out that morning. Told that bitch where to get off and to get the fuck away from me. But, no, I gave Marisol the wrong idea when we worked together for Bella Matrix. I led her on. Went to the parties with her in tow. I enjoyed the attention. I liked the high life. And what did it get me? People that I love and care about have been hurt because of her obsession, and now our little girl—"

A sob stole his voice as it wracked his body. The torment of heartbreak wove its way deep into my soul as he poured out his pain. He didn't see himself the way I saw him, the way we all saw him. Pain raked him with its sharp talons and put the fragmented pieces of his peace of mind under an incriminating microscope. All he could see while looking through that lens was guilt. His objectivity was gone, but I could help. It was my turn. Where he'd been my strength through this ordeal, I could now be his.

"I want you to listen to me. I want you to concentrate on my words and hear everything I say to you. Nothing—absolutely nothing—that you have ever done with Marisol, or anyone else for that matter, led to the kidnapping of our daughter. You need to believe what I'm saying. In every one of those instances, Marisol was the common denominator. No matter what anyone says, you and I know she's the one responsible for Lacey, me, Aimee, and Paige being hurt. I wouldn't be surprised if she had something to do with Blake's death. Did the fallout affect other people? Damn right it did, but she's to blame. This is where it stops. Marisol is a grown woman, responsible for her actions. She could have stopped this twisted vendetta of hers anytime she wanted. She's evil, and her vindictiveness and hatred are a poison we were forced to drink.

"Again, she had the power to stop this, and who cares if you partied with her in your modeling days? You were young and had a pocket full of money and no responsibilities. Full of piss and vinegar, as my grandmother would say. But you aren't responsible for her choices. She is. Her husband is as corrupt as she is and might have had something to do with this. If that's the case, we'll find our daughter and make them pay for what they've done, but, until then, we have to stay focused and do whatever is necessary to bring our baby home."

He looked at me with sad eyes. "I don't know how you can stand to look at me."

"The same way that you looked at me on the day I turned my back and ignored my daughter. By reminding you that you're human and humans make mistakes."

He wrapped his arms around me, burying his face in my hair. "I love you."

"And I love you. Anything could happen to anyone on any day. The simplest thing can trigger a tragic chain of events. I could never accuse you because you never accused me. Every day I cried and waited in the bedroom for you to come in and unleash the fury of hell on me. To blame me and to walk away from me and hate me forever. Yet you didn't. Instead every day you checked on me. Covered me with blankets, dried my tears, and made me drink water. You held me. All I wanted to do was crawl into a hole and die, and you refused to let me go. There's no way I'm going to let you blame yourself, just as you never let me take the blame."

I locked my fingers around his middle and held on for dear life. I didn't ever want to let him go. "We'll get through this. I tipped my chin up and leaned it against his chest to force him to look into my eyes. "We will bring our little girl home, Dec."

He squeezed me tightly. "And when we do," he said, his voice croaky and hoarse, "I'm never going to let either of you out of my sight."

Chapter 16

Over the past week, I found myself spending more time in the nursery. I wasn't sure why. The relationship that Teresa had formed with Eliana fascinated me because I didn't understand it. I had no memory of my mother having a connection, like the one they shared, with me.

The tiniest, simplest little thing would make the baby smile and laugh, and I found myself smiling as I watched them at play. All Teresa had to do was put her hands in front of her face and then pull them away saying peek-a-boo, and Eliana would let out a belly laugh. She was such a brave little girl. I admired that. Tentative at first, she adapted quickly. Her independent streak showed with her every effort to walk by herself. With each step, her confidence grew. It mattered not if she fell down. She merely picked herself back up and continued on. *Was I like that as a baby?*

No one could answer my questions. Instead, I became a voyeur, watching from the outside in to get a glimpse inside my daughter's world. Each day I moved physically closer to the two of them as they had playtime. I told myself I had no time for such foolish things. That Eliana had a role to play just as I did, and, individually, we would perfect them.

I did as Manny dictated, preparing myself to be by his side in my role as first lady, and told myself she would do the same. Once she was old enough to understand, she would have tutors and learn to ride horseback as well as other things that would be expected of her. Her fate would not be that of her namesake's, being given to a man with a predilection for young girls. No, my Eliana would be smart, beautiful, and worshipped as first daughter. But, today. . . today she was sweet and innocent and would have no memory of me not ruling her with a firm hand. Today I could merely enjoy her innocence. I couldn't recall ever experiencing that particular trait.

As I watched, it seemed that Eliana wanted to include me in her play. Her attempts to walk unassisted were rewarded by Teresa with every single step. The initiation of her quest was the same as the day before. First, she pulled herself up by holding onto Teresa's arms. Then Teresa, ever vigilant, placed her hands upon Eliana's waist, encircling it to steady her.

Once she was standing, she looked at me and smiled, and, despite my attempts at indifference, I gave a smile back to her. After all, it couldn't hurt. She would never remember it.

She looked down at her feet. First one step, then two, as she held fast to Teresa's hand. As she inched away, she grew unsteady, but it didn't deter her. She only paused, regained her balance, and took another step. If she were to come to me, it would be a four-step solo flight. *Will she do it today?*

I opened my hands, which had been folded on my lap. I didn't reach for Eliana, just placed my palms up in her direction. Her expression grew serious.

"No, no mi *princesita*. You are a brave girl today. Come. You can do it. *Ven a mi.*"

She studied me for a moment as if asking herself if she should trust me. Her leg lifted, toes pointed, and she took a step. By now she was only holding on to one of Teresa's fingers. Again, she steadied herself, but this time she let go of the safety of Teresa's index finger. She wobbled and concentrated on keeping herself upright. The next step was uncertain but taken alone. Her eyes widened as she realized she'd done what she'd set out to do. Her little legs stiffened, then she looked from her toes upward until her eyes met mine. "Ven a mi," I whispered. Come to me.

Challenge accepted, she kept her eyes locked with mine and took one, two, three . . . and plop!

She fell forward on her hands and knees. As she

looked up at me, her face turned red, and a determined little expression took control of her features. Seeing such a fierce look on such a little girl made me laugh.

"Try again, princesita. You'll do it eventually."

She stayed rooted to the floor on her hands and knees and crawled over to me so quickly I barely had time to blink. In a flash, she'd pulled herself up by climbing my legs. When she stood, her head was just at my knees. She locked her fingers onto my clothes, making small indentations in the material. Once she was sure she had a firm grip, she began bouncing up and down. She had so much to say as she babbled incessantly in a language only she could comprehend.

"What a brave and feisty girl you are, and so clever too. I like that."

I didn't like babies at all. They were messy, smelly little creatures that had not a thing to offer for all your efforts, but not her. Eliana was different because she amused me. Most little ones would've been afraid of me. Not her. She had the instincts of a survivor. I couldn't help but like her. She made me wonder if I might have possessed the same traits when I was a baby. Of course, I had no memory of that time. I also had no idea how to be a mother. Even though I watched my mother a few times with the younger children, I mostly ignored her. She always did what my father said without question. She was sad and weak. I never wanted to be like her, and, because of that, I kept my distance. Teresa gave me a better understanding of what it would take to connect with a child, and she wouldn't dare criticize me if I didn't get something right.

"I'll get her some juice." Teresa didn't give me time to object and was out the door before I had a chance to tell her to take the baby with her. Both Eliana and I watched as Teresa quickly left the room, both of us sensing this was not a good idea. And then we gave each other a blank stare.

It lasted for a few moments, neither one of us knowing what to make of the other. She blinked.

And blinked.

And blinked.

As I looked at her, I was in awe. Having been in the fashion and beauty industry for most of my adult life, I'd never appreciated the beauty of a natural, flawless complexion. Hers was a shade or two darker than porcelain and as smooth and buttery as the finest silk. Her eyes were evenly spaced from the bridge of her nose, bright, crystal blue, and beautifully round with long, sweeping black lashes. Her dark brown hair wasn't long, but framed her face perfectly, with soft tendrils that framed her cheeks. Her beauty was innocent and pure. The type of perfection that could never be gotten from a bottle, tube, or applicator. She was perfect.

Her knees began to wobble, though she was still latched onto my clothing. Without thinking, I held my hands out to her, and she let go and lifted her arms. I lifted her up, my hold tentative at best and, for an instant, I was glad that Teresa wasn't there to witness my awkwardness. Eliana looked me straight in the eye with no fear. Our faces were merely inches apart, and we eyed each other as we made our observations and conclusions. She was so serious.

"Well, little one. Do I meet with your approval?"

She gave me another look, blinked, and then turned her attention to my necklace. "So, you like jewelry, do you princesita?"

Eliana paid no attention to me and instead fisted the jeweled, gold chain that dripped with a five-carat emerald surrounded by diamonds. With both hands, she gleefully banged the chain against my throat and chest. Then she paused for a moment, inspected it, and lifted the gem to her mouth. *Is she going to eat it?*

"Easy!" My tone was louder and harsher than I'd spoken to her just moments ago. She stopped and froze in position with her mouth open, gem in her hand. She didn't move, but I detected a slight quiver of her bottom lip. Oh, no. She's going to scream.

Now it was my turn to become stone. I didn't move, stilled at the thought of this child screaming in my ear and no Teresa to take her from me. She hadn't yet returned with the bottle.

My posture locked in place. I had no idea what to do if this girl should let loose and pierce my eardrum. I couldn't put her down and go look for Teresa because, inevitably, that would trigger off the sound. *Shit! Shit! Shit!*

I decided the best thing to do was to stay exactly where I was and murder Teresa when she came back— after she gave the baby her juice. I stared at Eliana, and she stared at me. She hadn't moved, but her chest rose and fell with rapid breaths. It was like waiting for a dam to burst or a bomb to explode. The imaginary detonating device in my head ticking away the seconds while I waited for the imminent explosion, but just when I thought all was lost and she was going to cry no matter what I did, she stopped. Her shoulders slumped, and her body relaxed. As she yawned, I experienced the decompressing feel of stiffness leaving her little body. Her eyes softened, and her head tilted. Another yawn followed by a little smile. Her lids struggled to stay open, and she fell against me, her head resting on my shoulder as she moved against my chest. *Aw.*

Aw? What the hell is "aw"?

My spine stiffened as I reminded myself that I don't do babies. But she smelled so clean and sweet. But I was Marisol Franzi Vallega. I. Didn't. Do. Babies! But, but . . . No buts! Remember what this baby is for. Appearance is everything! This is all an illusion, and she is but a piece of a puzzle to get Manny and I to the presidenc—

Eliana rotated her shoulders and head and tucked herself under my chin. Was this what they called a snuggle? *Aw.*

No "aw"! Absolutely not!

I didn't move, refused even, but Eliana did. Positioning herself, she twisted her little baby body against mine for a more perfect fit than she had just moments ago. A million thoughts raced through my mind. I didn't want them; I didn't understand them. I shouldn't be having them.

I couldn't help it. No one was around to see me, so, just this once, I surrendered to feelings I didn't, and would probably never, understand. Eliana trusted me and she shouldn't. No one did. She should be careful of women like me. *But just this once . . .*

I closed my eyes, inhaling her sweet baby fragrance while momentarily allowing myself to sink into the strange warm feeling. I couldn't help but ask myself if this was what love was supposed to feel like? Soft and fuzzy? It was so . . . not me.

As Eliana's warm, wispy breaths skated against my neck, I stayed suspended in the moment. Like a lazy afternoon in a hammock, I involuntarily rocked, relishing whatever this was. I let it wash over me and soak in because I knew I might never feel it again. Eliana was as precious as a beautiful piece of ivory; a pawn in a chess game. And, if I wasn't careful, she could make an unpredictable, deadly move and capture the queen.

Chapter 17

Manny

Manny had been anticipating the call. After digging into the connections between ADDEX Pharmaceuticals and some highly visible businessmen and politicians, he had reservations about being connected to them. Senator Ford was on the board, and he rubbed him the wrong way. After their meeting in D.C., Manny hoped to sever their connection if there ever was one. Sure, he could be congenial should they wind up at the same public function, but beyond that, he thought it best to keep his distance from the slimy old bastard. All it took was one reporter, and that old man's empire would come tumbling down.

Kate Frampton was another story. What benefit

would there be to have a woman as a business associate? Of course, he could fuck her, but other than that there was no way he would answer to her. He wasn't foolish enough to think that in the future she wouldn't call in her favors, and he didn't take orders from any woman no matter how much money she offered.

The idea of owing anything to someone made no sense. Manny was a self-made man. Sure, Carlos had made him heir to the cartel, but he'd earned it. With every beating and murder committed, he'd shown his loyalty and worked his way up. Carlos wasn't a fool, and he had made Manny in his own image. He'd stripped him of all feeling while making him play that he cared. His acting ability surprised even himself; at every meeting and in every deal he showed compassion, but it was all superficial. If people didn't pay their debts with money, they settled with skin, and he had no remorse about it. Kate could take ADDEX and stick it up her ass. He didn't need her.

His cell phone rang. Speak of the devil. "Hello, Kate."

"Manny. We haven't heard from you."

"I've been busy. The adoption came through rather quickly after our meeting. A little girl. We've been adjusting to family life."

"Yes. I hoped you liked our gift. How is your lovely family?"

Gift? "As surprised as we were at how quickly

events transpired, they're all fine. Thank you for asking." The words warned and snapped like the tail end of a whip. It seemed odd that this woman would be injecting herself in such a personal matter. "What's the purpose of the call, Kate?"

"Well, I haven't heard from you, and the senators mentioned they haven't as well. Considering that I made you a solid offer, I'd have thought you'd have an answer by now."

"I do. It just wasn't on my list of priorities."

"I'm sorry to hear that. Perhaps your priorities need a bit of adjusting."

What a bitch. "Don't overstep, Kate. It doesn't look good on you."

"I overstep all the time, Manny, especially in matters that are beneficial to ADDEX—and I do it in only the most expensive shoes," she laughed. "But I digress; the clock is ticking on our offer. This call is to let you know that it's about to expire. We need an answer."

Fucking bitch! She presumed he owed her something, and he didn't like her tone. She didn't know it, but she was only confirming the correctness of his decision to decline the offer. The only thing she might have been good for was a quick fuck while he was in the States, but she just killed that thought for him. No way would he be her puppet. He'd choke her with the strings first. Wrap the cords around her throat and smile into her face as she turned beautiful colors as her breath left her body.

"Then you shall have it; the answer is no."

The pregnant pause stretched a little longer than he'd expected. Maybe he was the first person to refuse help from ADDEX. Perhaps he was in the minority because he had no desire for a charitable cock suck. Whatever. His answer was final. The last thing he needed was some corporate bitch dictating his actions and decisions. He used women to further his agenda, not the other way around.

"I think you should reconsider. ADDEX's arm of influence extends much further than you know. We don't extend offers lightly and take it very personally when someone refuses our goodwill."

Apparently, his answer wasn't firm enough. "You make that sound like a threat, Ms. Frampton—and I take those very personally."

"We don't make threats, Manny, only promises. You're climbing the mountain of politics with no experience behind you. I can assure you the path up is rocky and unsteady. The senators and I are merely trying to help you reach your goals. Better men than you have accepted our help and are now sitting exactly where they want to be."

"A puppet presidency? No, thanks. I'll pass."

In the few months since their meeting, he'd decided his own resources from within the cartel were the only ones he needed, and he had complete control of them. Laundering money wasn't a new profession, and cartel connections assured loyalty. He calculated the benefit of having senators Bushman and Ford in his pocket and, as long as they were connected to the deal that ADDEX offered, they were of no use to him. No matter. If he needed pocket politicians, the United States had a big pool from which to choose.

"I'll give you a little time to rethink your position because, apparently, you don't yet appreciate what we can do for you. Our marketing is a powerful beast and can make you into a saint or a sinner in the court of public opinion. You have seventy-two hours."

Click.

He stared at the phone. The pompous little bitch had hung up on him. Fine. She wanted control, but he took it back. He would take his chances with the devil he knew. He controlled the underbelly in a third of the world and, if ADDEX didn't watch their step, he had the technology to infiltrate their mainframe and wreak a little havoc just to have fun.

A knock on the door interrupted his violent thoughts. "Come in."

"Buenas tardes, Manny. Ocupado?"

César was Marianna's uncle, but Manny regarded him his family as well. A well-spoken, fit, and attractive older man, Manny had known the man ever since he was a child when Carlos had brought him into the organization. He was sure César resented that it was Manny behind the desk and not the other way around.

After all, the older man had the benefit of experience, was Carlos's brother, and should have been the one to take over the business after his death. Of course, César would have run things the old way. Manny didn't share the old world vision of using guns, bombs, and blades. His goal was to bring the family business into the future, and that required information technology. Even now he was recruiting the savviest hackers out there, had his own cybersecurity team, and had spent millions on cutting edge protection. He had more than enough safety measures in place, but he wanted more. All it took was money. Everyone had a price.

As César took a seat, he scanned the room, his eyes filled with lust. Manny enjoyed witnessing the look, knowing the man was parched for the power he held and would love to knock him off his throne. His office was his command post. Who wouldn't like to direct and command from this room? It reeked of power. The furnishings were masculine, sporting wing-backed chairs of oxblood leather. A massive fireplace took up one-third of the outside wall. Above the thick, oak mantle hung Fernando Botero's *The Kiss of Judas*. It was a constant reminder to him that no matter how many faithful followed him, it only took one man to cut down a king.

Manny went to the bar and poured a splash of Pappy Van Winkle into two rocks glasses. It would take the edge off the anger he'd felt since his conversation with Kate. It was a particular favorite of his, and he regularly had it shipped to him from the United States. He handed the glass to César. To his dismay, the man downed it in one gulp.

"What you just threw back is the finest Kentucky bourbon. You should savor it. Appreciate the complexity."

Carlos shrugged. "It all does the same thing if you drink enough of it—numbs the soul."

Manny shook his head. César wasn't much different from Carlos. Both had the means to indulge in the most beautiful material possessions, yet neither had an appreciation for any of the finer things. Carlos had chosen the right person to replace him. César treated Manny as an ignorant pig, but he kept the older man close. He held a high and commanding position within the cartel, and Manny had placed him there. César believed it was Manny's way of honoring a man whose ascension as king of the drug empire was diverted by a resentful brother, but his reasons were much more personal. César was dirty, therefore the perfect scapegoat. If ever any law enforcement infiltrated the cartel, Manny could deny affiliation. His business was real estate, as far as the public knew. Should the house of white powder topple, his hands were clean. He would swear to dismantle the drug problem of his country. It was another political platform where one hand could feed the other.

César's chin dropped low, creating another chin above his thick neck. He cocked his head and looked up at Manny. "We had some difficulty today. At the estate."

A scowl darkened Manny's expression. "What kind of difficulty?"

César shrugged. "I stopped by to see Marianna and the girl."

"My daughter," Manny corrected him.

"Yes. Your daughter. She was outside with Marianna."

"Outside? I told her not to go outside until our defense system was completely installed. Is it?"

"No. Another week or two. They're working on it." The older man gave an indifferent shrug. "I told her to go inside, but she said the baby needed air." He looked up, a challenging look in his eye. "If her father were alive, he would beat that sass out of her. I could help."

Manny responded with a determined look. "No one touches my wife."

Unconsciously, Manny's hands had tightened into balled fists.

A condescending smile played at César's lips. "Calm down, Manny. No one would dare. Including me."

Manny kept a rein on the anger that bubbled inside, though it was nearing a boiling point. "So what was the problem today?

César raised a brow while an arrogant snarl hooked his lip. "Drones."

Chapter 18

D eclan

"Wow. Like the new office." Declan took a seat at a conference table in the new MarSin Falcon offices. Though it wasn't as elaborate as his own company, The Studio, it was a whole lot nicer than the small home office where the business started. "When is everyone supposed to get here?"

"It's just Fal. He should be here soon."

"I'm happy for you, bro. I wasn't sure what direction you were going in, but I'm glad you found something to make you happy—personally and professionally."

Declan looked like he'd aged twenty years. Tired eyes, a forced smile, sunken posture—he barely resembled the vibrant face of men's cologne, clothing, and health magazines. Although months might not seem a long time, when you were grieving the loss of a loved one it had the same physical effect as several years.

"Can I get you something to drink?"

Declan laughed. "It's too early in the day for what I really want."

"Is Aria with Aimee?"

"Yeah. She wanted to come with me, but Aimee convinced her that this was just a briefing and we'd fill her in on everything once we got back to your house."

Declan and Aria had come up to Deep Creek this time around, but Carter had to do something to provide a change of atmosphere. Though he thought it would be of little help, it wasn't doing them any good staying at home. Since he knew he wasn't getting the full story from his brother, he'd called Aria's mother, Jeannie. She'd told him that the two of them walked around the house like zombies most of the time. Frequent visits to Karas's bedroom resulted in Aria's tears and Declan's increasing sadness. With everything the two of them had been through they'd remained resolute, but he couldn't help but wonder if this would be the thing that broke them. Their daughter—the very person who had given them joy and purpose—had taken with her both her mother and father's hearts and a piece of everyone else's who knew her. Grief, in its many forms, changed people and relationships. Even if they recovered Karas and brought her home—check that, *when* they rescued Karas and brought her home—life would never be the same. Declan and Aria would be wary of everyone that looked at their daughter. There would be no more "what a pretty baby," or "your little girl is adorable," statements, and the like, that wouldn't be suspect. Superficial comments would be held under a magnifying glass. Carter only hoped it didn't change them too much. If they didn't keep it in check, the paranoia that could result would steal just as much, or more, from them as had been already.

The door opened and closed. Falcon joined them in the conference room.

"Let's dispense with the formalities and get started." Carter rose from the table, and a confused Declan followed suit.

"Where are we going? I thought the meeting was here."

"We use this room for meeting with clients. We're going where we can dig into this a little deeper."

They walked into the next room, to a closet door—or at least it looked like a closet door. When Falcon turned the handle and opened it, a small elevator was revealed. He followed Carter inside. Falcon was the last one in. He pulled the door closed, shifted a gate all the way to the left, and pushed an unmarked button. Declan could tell they were going down, and a minute later it stopped.

They exited the elevator just as quickly as they'd

entered. Declan's eyes widened as he looked around the room. "What is this?"

"This, my brother, is the heart and soul of MarSin Falcon's international operations."

Pride threaded Carter's words as he moved toward a table more significant than the one upstairs. Ten chairs graced the rectangular piece of oak. In the middle of the tabletop was a circle with a large, Roman "X" in the middle. The words arched above and below the "X" read "No innocent forsaken; no evil unavenged."

Declan made a half turn as he moved toward a chair. To his right was a wall outfitted with about twenty monitors. At the moment, only half were filled with images from unknown places. It looked like something the government might have in a classified location.

Falcon and Carter took a seat at the table, and Declan followed suit. "I'm not sure I understand. I thought this was a computer security company." Confusion clouded his eyes and reverberated in his statement.

You're inside the head operations room for our global division. Our teams operate secretly. Most of our people are military trained, but we also contract experts in every field. We use their talents to infiltrate where we would, otherwise, stand out. They gather intel, we go in with muscle. Our mission is to get the job done while operating under the radar. Then guys like me come in and finish the job. If it weren't for your daughter's situation, you wouldn't even know this part of our company exists. Most of our people look like your neighbor, doctor, or teacher. They go to work and come home every day just like you do. Nothing appears unique about them, but they are experts in their fields, problem solvers if you will, and they believe in justice. It's easier for them to get in and out when they can masquerade as part of a group. The goal is not to be discovered, just provide intel so we can solve problems.

Declan's head was spinning. He made a quick mental note to discuss this at another time with his brother. Right now, he only wanted their company, or the X Force, or whoever in the hell they were, to use all this mission control bullshit to bring home his little girl.

Falcon sat his take-out coffee, a pad with notes on it, and a laptop on the table. "The current intel is as recent as yesterday. Marcus and his team were able to plant two small surveillance devices on the ground. Vallega's house is heavily guarded. He has two men posted at every entrance, and they change shifts every four hours. Three iron gates lead to the property. Not only does he have security coded keypads at the entrances, but he also has three men patrolling the areas around the gates. We needed a diversion so our men could plant the cameras. We used drones."

Chapter 19

A ria

"Are you okay?"

I looked up at Aimee, thankful to have her for a friend and sister-in-law. Living with the Sinclair men had its challenges, but we were glad we had them. Declan and Carter would do anything for their loved ones. I could only hope they could pull off a miracle and bring Karas back home.

I sat cross-legged on the floor of the guest bedroom, looking at the pile of scattered pictures. Bits and pieces of happy memories. I wouldn't dare leave home without a picture of my baby. Though I had hundreds on my phone, I had nearly as many in print. With a father whose livelihood depended on a camera, there was always one close by our little girl.

Aimee sat down beside me, picking up one photo at the corner. She turned it this way and that as she looked at it from different angles.

"I don't think there's a bad angle on that little one. She's so photogenic. That face. Those eyes. And that smile!"

I angled my head, leaning over to see which picture she referred to. "Oh, that one. Yep. She was a character that day. I had taken her to The Studio. We were meeting Declan for lunch. One of the photographers, Jon, had a cancellation. When he came into the office to tell Declan that one of his appointments needed to reschedule, he fell in love with Karas. She had him completely charmed within ten minutes, and he asked us if he could take her picture. She was such a little ham. No tears. No hesitation. She took to the camera as easily as her daddy."

I clung to the memory, wrapping it with my love and holding it close to my heart. I no longer felt anxious or sad, just numb. It wasn't acceptance that Karas was gone, for I would never let her go, even if I never again held her in my arms. She would forever be mine. Her laughter traveled through my bloodstream giving me the hope that she would return. I still believed that we'd see her again. I had to.

"They shouldn't be too long. They're meeting Falcon. I'm not sure what they're planning, but I've seen for myself, when most have given up, they come through."

Aimee put her arm around my shoulder as she offered me hers. I took the invitation, lying my head down and closing my eyes. I was so tired. Every day it was an effort to simply breathe. My body moved through invisible pools of water, resistant to each step forward with limbs weighted with grief. All I wanted to do was sleep. I wanted it to be a bad dream, hoping that at any moment I'd wake up to see eyes that looked like mine.

"Why don't you go lay down for a little while? I'll tell him to wake you as soon as he gets back."

I nodded. Sleep was something I couldn't seem to get enough of. I pushed myself off the floor. "I'll be down soon. Just a short nap."

Aimee was now standing. She had retrieved an empty wicker basket from the bureau and was collecting the pictures. Once she placed the pile in the basket, she set it on the nightstand beside me.

As I burrowed into the soft mattress and plush, blue comforter, exhaustion slayed me. "Thanks, Aim. I'll see you in a bit."

As Aimee closed the door behind her, my gaze went to the basket. It was painted a soft eggshell color, trimmed in the same pale blue as the bedding. I reached out, put my hand in the basket, and retrieved one of the pictures. As I pulled it near, I recognized it as one that Declan had taken. One of me rocking Karas when she was just a few weeks old.

The photo was in black and white, but I remembered the scene in color. Karas liked to kick her legs about. She didn't like the confinement of sleepers, so we put her in long nightgowns. When she slept, we'd cinch the bottom so it couldn't bunch around her and could also keep her warm, but when she was awake, and in my arms, I would loosen the tie, and the infant dance recital would begin. On this particular day, she seemed deep in thought. Our eyes locked, drawn together like magnets, we stared into each other's souls. Mother and daughter. The perfect connection. A never-ending bond. I traced the smooth image of her head with my finger, remembering how she'd grown so sleepy that day. Freshly diapered and nursed, she was still nuzzled against my breast as I rocked her ever so gently.

I closed my eyes and recalled the moment. Its everlasting imprint became clear in my thoughts. My senses engaged. I was no longer at Carter and Aimee's house. I was at home in the nursery. It was a warm day. The soft crash of waves could be heard through the window. I could see Karas. Smell her. Feel her. My heart responded to the memory. The constant shaking of my insides quelled. My shoulders relaxed. Achy limbs fell heavy into the mattress. My pulse slowed to a more calm and leisurely pace. A peaceful tune began to play in my memory, at first very faint. I pulled the photograph into my chest, holding it close to better feel the connection. The sound of the melody increased, and I began to hum the song I'd sung to Karas as she'd fallen asleep. A song my grandmother sang to all her babies, and her grandbabies. One that her mother sang to her.

Hmmm hmm hmm . . . hmm hm hm hm hm . . .
Just a simple little ditty, in her good old Irish way,
And I'd give the world to hear her sing
That song to me today.

Too-ra-loo-ra-loo-ral,
too-ra-loo-ra-li,
too-ra-loo-ra-loo-ral,
hush now don't you cry.

"Please come home, my sweet girl," I whispered. "Mommy needs you."

Chapter 20

M anny

MANNY'S HAND balled into a fist. "And what did the drones see?"

"Nothing much. A truck." César's reckless indifference grated on Manny's nerves.

"A truck?"

"A truck filled with purified water. It was nothing." César hunched his shoulders in a quick shrug. "Of course, the bottom was hollowed out and carried about three million in cocaine."

"Why would a truck be at my home? I've told you to keep that shit off-site."

"I had a delivery for you, also at the bottom of the

truck. I had it taken through the private entrance to the dungeon. No one saw a thing."

"All right. Marianna never goes there. She thinks of it as smelly and dirty just because of the name. It shouldn't have been a problem if it was concealed well when you brought it in, and whoever was controlling those drones . . ."

César looked toward the door. "Except that our men fired at the drones. It might have drawn attention. You know, seemed suspicious."

"God damn it, César!" Manny's closed fist met the desktop with a solid punch. "You should have been in control of the men. Don't they know when—and when not—to react? Idiots! They raise suspicion when they behave this way!" He pushed off the desk, pacing in circles as he contemplated what to do next. His eyes darkened to a soulless black, and a scowl veiled his features. The control he had been hanging onto by a thread snapped. He turned to César, all semblance of humanity evaporating before the older man's eyes.

"Bring them to me. All of them." His tone was deadly.

Secretly César enjoyed watching Manny give in to his primal nature. He needed incidents like this to build a case against him. "Manny. Be reasonable."

Manny slammed his fist down again. "I said, bring them to me!"

"Now calm down," he said, appearing to do damage control. César leaned forward. "They were just boys being boys. You remember what that was like, don't you? Just a little target practice. Harmless, really."

"Harmless is not how I see it. They drew attention —negative attention. It could harm us!"

César stood and took a few steps until he was next to his rival. If he didn't think it would get him killed, he'd plunge a knife into Manny's heart right now. He was a patient man and had other plans. If he could incite Manny's anger more frequently, eventually, he would lose control completely. Then César would take his rightful place.

"*Miho* . . ." César placed a hand on his shoulder, speaking in a soothing tone. "I'll take care of it. That's my job." César knew Manny hated the touch of a man. He'd been forced to endure much of it when he was a boy. Another one of his brother's desensitization methods. He remembered it well.

"I have a little something that will take the edge off; the gift I had delivered to you yesterday. I thought you'd find it when you went into the dungeon."

Manny looked up at the man with disgust. The older man removed his hand as he tipped his chin toward the door.

"Come with me." César walked toward the door. Sensing Manny wasn't behind him, he looked over his shoulder. "Come on. What I have to show you will make you feel better."

Manny followed reluctantly. He hadn't checked

the security feed from yesterday. No one had alerted him to the delivery, but, then, no one had told him about the drones. If he was walking into a trap . . .

"Don't look so grave, Manny," César interrupted. "We're only going down to the gym."

The mention of the gym piqued his interest. He needed some way to work off the murderous rage infiltrating his usual calm. It was down on the lowest level, in the dungeon. Filled with the latest exercise equipment, it included a basketball court and a boxing ring. It also served much darker purposes, especially for those who were caught doing something that could taint Manny's name or damage cartel business.

They didn't speak in the elevator, but once on the lower level, César pointed toward the private changing room. "Go. I have a surprise for you."

"Is it you? Did you set up something special for you and me?" A snarl competed with Manny's salacious gaze. "If you wanted to spar, you didn't need to go through all this trouble to surprise me. All you had to do was ask. I've been wanting to get you in the ring. It would be a pleasure to kick your ass."

A laugh rushed out of the older man. "Not me. I'm an old man. What fun would that be for you? Trust me, what I have for you will last a little longer."

A few minutes later Manny returned. A satisfied smile appeared on César's face as he motioned with a crooked finger for Manny to follow him. They went in the direction of the boxing ring where a muffled sound was heard. He couldn't identify it at first, but what he saw when they rounded the half wall that separated them from their destination, pleased him. It was just what he needed.

The chain was thick and sturdy, easily holding the burden of weight below it.

"Your gloves." Manny kept his eyes fixed in front of him as he held out his hands.

César held the gloves as Manny pushed his hands inside. First one, then the other. They resembled sparring gloves except for a leather strip across the knuckle embedded with metal studs. Once César had tightened the final knot, Manny began bouncing and punching his knuckles together. It was perfect. Exactly what he needed.

Satisfaction washed over the old man's face as a sinister smile played at his lips. "I knew you'd like it," César said. "I'll leave you alone to enjoy."

Manny listened as the man's steps faded in the distance but didn't make a move until he heard the door click behind him. The old man was right. He did know precisely what Manny needed.

His fist flew through the air. The whooshing sound feeding the animal inside of him. His heartrate ratcheted, his pulse jackhammering as the blood rushed through his veins. The feeling was euphoric, flooding his ears with a symphony of two sounds: his beating heart and a woman's scream.

Chapter 21

M anny

His frustrations vented, Manny showered, changed, and returned to his office. César had been waiting inside. "I thought you left."

"I would have except I received a very unusual call. One that concerns you."

Manny noted that of all the chairs in his office, César was sitting in the one behind his desk. Walking over to it, he stared down at the older man. "You mind?"

César rose slowly. The two men locked gazes for a stuttered moment, and then César removed himself from Manny's chair to take a different seat.

Manny sat and looked over at Marisol's uncle, a silent warning in his eyes.

"Tell me about ADDEX Pharmaceuticals." César held Manny's gaze with a determined one of his own.

"There isn't anything to tell. They wanted to be a supporter of my campaign. I declined."

"I don't think that was a wise move."

"I don't remember asking you."

A silent war of wills accompanied the tension in the air, and César drew first blood.

"You don't know who you're messing with, hijo. Carlos wouldn't have turned down an opportunity to do business with a giant. You must think of the future of the business. Right now the big drug is oxy. Pharmaceuticals control the price of legal distributions, but we can get five times the price they charge. There will be more opportunity for us as more addictive drugs are developed. Consider the cost of your refusal. It would tie our hands if we refuse to play ball with ADDEX. We should be expanding influences that would benefit the drug business."

"I don't care." Manny's resented being second-guessed. "I met with the head of the company, and not by my choosing. The meeting was sprung on me when I went to D.C. I heard the woman out, weighed the risks and benefits, and decided to decline her offer."

César gave Manny a questioning look. "She made this offer while you met with the president? Can't you see, that was a clear indication that politicians would turn a blind eye to your business with her. There's a trickle-down effect here; they turn a blind eye and so does every branch of government and law enforcement under them. Carlos had waited for something like this for a long time. If he were here he would have jumped at the chance to get into bed with ADDEX. How stupid can you be?"

Manny tolerated César's presence for the sake of peace. When Carlos died there were many within the organization who wanted to see César succeed his brother. They resented, and quietly ignored, Carlos's directive that Manny be the one to take his place. Little by little Manny was winning them over, but things like that took time. No matter, he was a patient man, but the blatant disregard for his authority caused his blood to once again boil. He would exercise his authority. He'd paid with his flesh and blood to earn his position, and he'd be damned if he'd let some old bastard tell him how he should run the company.

He picked up his cell phone from the desk. Scrolling through his most recent calls, he stabbed a finger to the screen. It only took a moment to connect.

"Manny. So good to hear from you." Kate Frampton's tone was smooth, creamy, and condescending.

"I'm calling about your offer."

"I thought you would be. I look forward to doing business with you."

"That's just it; we won't be. I don't need a few days

to think it over. I have already. The answer is definitely no."

"You sound angry, Manny. How unprofessional of you."

"I'm not angry, just determined. I don't know what you've heard about me, or why you'd think I'd want any part of your offer. I think you need it more than I do. I see it for what it is, Kate, and I don't like the plan. It benefits you more than it does me."

"I'll accept your decision, Manny, but, before I do, I'd like to give you one more chance. The time hasn't run out. Perhaps speak with your advisors."

Confirmation. That was all he needed. The moment Kate said advisors he knew César had played a part in this. It wouldn't go unpunished.

"No one speaks for me, and my decision remains the same. The answer is no."

Manny didn't wait to hear the rest of what Kate would say and didn't want to waste his breath on her anymore. The bad mood he'd worked off in the gym had returned with a vengeance. His heart rate, now elevated, drummed in his ears, and his jaw ached from clenching. César had always been an arrogant prick. He needed to learn a lesson about boundaries. No one crossed the line between suggestions and orders other than him. Manny breathed deeply. He would deal with the old man in his own time and in his own way.

"So, there you have it, *tío*. All's well that ends well, so they say. ADDEX is no longer a concern of mine, therefore it isn't a concern of yours, but then again, it never was. I have some things to attend to and you have security issues. There's no more to discuss." Manny looked down at a pile of paperwork and pulled a few single sheets from the pile. César was dismissed without a word.

César had remained quiet all through the entire conversation, knowing that Manny had put the call on speaker for his benefit. "The final decision was always yours. I was only playing devil's advocate." César stood. "I'm going home. A good meal and some sleep are what I need. You should try to get some too."

Manny didn't say a word, instead he tried to distance himself from his festering anger while he continued with the business at hand. César exited the room, closing the office door behind him, and as he walked down the hallway a satisfied smile inched onto his lips.

He pulled his cell phone from his pocket, hit one number, and placed it to his ear. "It's me. Everything worked beautifully. He's out and doesn't have a clue. Send the pictures."

Chapter 22

M anny

It had been a very long day, and Manny was tired. The more he thought about the day's events the angrier he became. The security system he'd approved, which protected them with technology, and the men he and Cesar had picked to guard the house were superior marksmen. The last thing Manny needed were drones hovering over the property—his property.

Privacy was his primary concern. He didn't like the feds getting up close and personal with him. That was one of the reasons he decided to back off from the pharmaceutical company. His meeting with Senators Ford and Bushman made him uneasy. Although he'd worked with Bushman before, Ford was a new acquaintance.

His gut told him to stay away from that man, and he trusted his instincts. The last thing he needed to get into was a pissing contest with American politicians.

Manny strode through the hallway with determined steps. His muscles were tight. After his work out earlier some of the tension had drained from his body, but the combination of the drones, Mariana's uncle, and his conversation with Kate Frampton, had him thirsting for blood once again. His fingers dug into his palms as his hands as he balled them into fists. He would achieve his goals and become the president of Colombia, but the road to legitimacy was paved with traitors. What he needed now was a drink and a good night's sleep.

The vibration in his pocket diverted his train of thought. He looked at the display. *What the hell does she want?*

"I've said everything I needed to say, Kate."

"Is that the way you greet everyone?" Sarcasm laced her tone.

"Just get to the point. What do you want?" Worn and threadbare, Manny's patience to deal with people had reached its limit.

"I wanted to inform you that I have contacted the senators. They are the gentlemen who set up the meeting for you when you came to the states. Now that you've declined our offer the senators have expressed to me that if you're not willing to work with one of the largest companies in the United States, they aren't willing to work with you. It looks bad, you know? Offering assistance and political aid to a prominent figure who's associated with illegal drugs, prostitution, human trafficking, and racketeering doesn't look good."

"I would say I'm surprised but I expected as much. People have been talking about me for years, but they have no proof because I have no involvement with such things."

"I'd agree with you, but some nasty information has come to light about you, Manny, especially in regard to the expansion of your family. I hope you, being the upstanding citizen you present yourself to be, can clear it up."

"What are you talking about? We did everything by the book."

"That would explain it. The fine print in that book you so casually reference had the power to resurrect or bury you. I gave you options, and you chose to dig your own grave. And speaking of reading, you might want to read the paper. Good luck to you, Manny. You're going to need it."

Kate hung up on him, leaving Manny to wonder what her cryptic message was about. He didn't have to wait long. Kate sent Manny a photo of a newspaper. It was the New York Times. Manny didn't routinely read the newspapers from the United States, especially within the last few months. He'd been concentrating his efforts on the brass ring of the presidency. He tapped his finger to the screen, and then with thumb and middle finger he widened the image. The headline read, "Fashion industry model pleads for the return of his missing daughter."

The phone buzzed as another image was received. Once again, he tapped the screen. The image was of a baby girl dressed in a white dress. *That fucking bitch!* Another photo came through, and this time it was Marianna outside of their home sitting on the lawn with the baby. His heart sped up as a laundry list of federal charges made an image in his head, the first of which was kidnapping. Eliana Vallega and Karas Sinclair were one and the same.

Chapter 23

Teresa watched me as I held Eliana. If I was going to pull off the act of doting mother, I had to get Eliana to trust me. It wasn't such a hardship. The moment I felt tired, Teresa took over. I'd been practicing small things like holding her and teaching her to wave. For two days in a row Teresa, Eliana, and I had gone outside to enjoy the beautiful weather. Teresa had brought along a blanket. We'd laid it out on the thick grass where Eliana ate some puffy treats while she looked at and listened to the birds. It didn't provide the same pleasure for me as a shopping trip, but I did enjoy watching her. Honestly, I didn't understand it at all. Perhaps it was just because it was a more peaceful experience than all the events we'd attended before Eliana had arrived. Those were mentally exhausting, and these times—like now—stirred something inside of me that made me happy.

When I looked down, Eliana was smiling at me. She pulled herself up by holding onto my legs. She was still shaky but doing better at walking every day. Once stabilized, she held one chubby little arm up to me.

"What do you want, princesita?" I bent over to lift her up; the sweet smell of innocence caressed my nose. She looked right into my eyes as she studied me, and a warm feeling wrapped around us both. I relaxed into its odd embrace. Eliana was the only living thing that gave my constant cynicism a time-out. She had no agenda, no ulterior motive. I could never remember a time when I didn't have to watch my back. Time spent with her was different. To get to know her was to understand purity.

The door to the nursery flew open. Startled, the three of us froze in place. Manny was angry. He wore his anger like a suit of armor, cutting through the peaceful feeling we'd cultivated within these walls. Violence resounded through the room, its weighty silence dictating the rapid beat of my heart. Having no care for the baby in my arms, he crossed the room and grabbed the back of my head.

"I thought you understood my instructions."

He forced my neck into a painful arch. The deadly look in his eyes stole my breath. I swallowed the lump in my throat, the ability to speak nearly failing me. "Let me go. I have no idea what you're talking about."

It was an effort to speak and not trip over my fear, but I refused to let him see the terror I felt inside. He released me, flinging me away and nearly making me lose my balance. Eliana started to cry.

Manny ran his hands over his face. I dared not move. He walked in agitated circles. "All you had to do was listen to my instructions, Marianna. But, no, you always have to do exactly as you want just to show that you can defy me."

"Calm down—"

"Calm down? I can't calm down. You went outside when I gave you explicit instructions not to."

"But she's fine. There's nothing wrong with her. She's adapted very well."

"Someone took pictures," he said through gritted teeth.

"So? We were going to take her out and show the world our perfect family façade. You know the paparazzi are everywhere. It's just a fact of life." I swayed, shushing Eliana to brave the building tension. I looked over at Manny who was still walking in circles. "You should go. Come back when you've calmed down."

He stopped moving. "Go? You're dismissing me?"

In a flash, he crossed the room and closed his hand around the top of my arm. "You'd better remember your place, Mariana. All it would take is a phone call, and I'll have your ass back in the nut house!"

Eliana rebelled at my unbalance. Manny's rough treatment unsettled us both. Frightened, she screamed as she tried to get out of my grasp. Her head turned this way and that, her arms reaching out for Teresa, who was too terrified to move.

Anger bubbled inside of me as I reined in my breathing. Control was a valuable commodity. He had none, and mine was quickly waning. I slowed my words, schooling them into an even pace. "You need to leave. You want this baby to like you in public? Let her see you when you're civil."

"You don't tell me what to do!" He pinched my chin between his fingers, a battlefield in the space between our eyes. I struggled to hold the baby tight. She'd come completely undone, her shrieks piercing my ears.

"*Aaaaahhh!*" Manny released his hold with a snapping motion, his orbital ritual now closer than ever. I took a step back. Eliana's horror-filled cries were bouncing off the wall. She straddled my hip as her head whipped around to find a safe place. The shrill sound unnerved Manny. He grew more agitated with each step.

"Make her stop."

"Then leave." It was a war of wills. I knew that if I showed any fear Manny would have the advantage and I refused to give up the ground of the one room in this house I had claimed. This room was our place of solace in the crazy world of unlawful acts. I hadn't realized it until that moment, but Teresa and this baby were all I had. I'd be damned if Manny would take it away from me. My father had stripped me of emotion, leaving nothing but a stone shell of the woman I could have become. Manny couldn't have whatever humanity was left of me. It was mine.

I looked to Eliana, ignoring him, and saw his black look in my peripheral vision. "*Cálmete*, princesita. Everything will be alright."

"Prin-ce-sita?" He grabbed me again, and this time strands of hair ripped from my scalp. Manny took a step around me, pinning me to at him as he looked down into my eyes. "So, does that make you the queen, mi amor?" His words were slow and deliberate, a threat hurled with every syllable. Eliana screamed louder than before, twisting and turning until I thought my arm would break.

"Get off me!" I demanded.

Manny let go and took one step away from me, but it was enough distance that I could give Teresa a pleading look. She understood, attempting to close the gap between us and take Eliana. Her eyes widened in silent warning, and I turned to see the back of Manny's hand flying through the air toward the baby with furious force.

Whap!

"Shut that little bitch up!"

Chapter 24

D eclan

DECLAN'S HEAD WAS SPINNING. X Force? Drones? He gave Carter a blank look. "I don't know what to do here. First, we come down to something like CIA headquarters, and then you're talking about my little girl in the same sentence as spy shit. This is all too much."

"I'm insulted. We're better than the CIA and much better looking." Falcon's attempt at humor earned him a death glare from Carter.

"I know it is, but wouldn't you rather have people like us to help with this? It's Karas's best chance. Local police can't do what we do."

Declan searched his brother's face and found truth and sincerity. "Do you know for sure they have her?"

"Look at this." Falcon pulled out eight by ten black and white photos and placed them in front of Declan. "This is from yesterday. While Vallega's men were busy with the drones, our guys placed surveillance cameras around the compound—and it is a compound. The dude is so paranoid he's got a mini army. After all the hoopla calmed down, we caught this image a few hours after."

Declan studied the images. Marisol was walking beside a shorter, older woman, and that woman was holding up a little girl. Karas! "Oh my God! She's alive."

The words rushed out. A quiet shout as the breath left Declan's body and caressed his daughter's name. He looked at the two men. "Are you positive? I mean, it looks like her."

"Here." Falcon gave him another photo—a closeup.

"She's gotten so big." Declan stared unabashedly at the photo while an errant tear spilled. "My baby girl." He looked up, a death grip on the image. "When can you go get her?"

"It's not that easy," Falcon said.

"Fuck that shit! Go get my daughter!" Suddenly combative, Declan unleashed on Falcon. "You've got all the big, bad guys on your team. If they're already there placing cameras and shit, they can bust the door down and take her."

"And possibly get her killed? No, thanks. I don't want your daughter's blood on my hands."

Declan sprung from the chair and lunged across the table at Falcon. He'd cocked his fist, aiming for Falcon's face when Carter intervened. He grabbed Declan's wrist and twisted, rendering it immobile. Declan's body turned, following the source of the pain.

"Knock it off." Carter's voice was a roar. "Just calm the fuck down and take a seat."

Reluctantly, Declan returned to his seat but never took his eyes off Falcon.

"Falcon, Marcus, and their team are our best assurance that we'll not only get Karas back but get her back in one piece." Carter waited while his brother regained his composure. "Look, I know you're pissed and you need someone to take all of this out on. Do it later. Fal's not the enemy. Vallega is."

Falcon leaned into the table. "Look, man. I know my method doesn't give you the warm fuzzies, but I want you back with your girl. Vallega is bad news. The feds have been trying to get him for years, but nothing's ever stuck. I'll be the first one to admit that I want to take him down, but I didn't want your daughter to be the reason. Hell, I wish that little girl was home with her momma just as much as you, but give us a chance to do our job. All this shit you see here? The spy shit you called it? It's going to work its cyberspace magic and help us get her. So, fuck any preconceived notions you had about the regular cop on the beat putting on a superhero cape and saving the day. This is real life, and Vallega is as dirty as they come. You don't want to know half the shit this guy's involved in. We're the best chance you've got to track down Karas and bring her back to you and Aria."

Carter silently drummed his fingers on the table as he waited for Declan to digest the scope of the mission. His brother was struggling. He could see it all over his face. He was chewing his bottom lip, and his hands were folded on the table with such a grip he thought he might snap a finger. Carter's gut twisted at seeing his brother so tormented, but this was something Declan had to be on board with, because the outcome might not have favorable results.

Finally, Declan faced Falcon. "My brother wouldn't be in business with you if he didn't trust you. I respect his judgment, and I'm sorry I almost punched you. You're right; all this stuff scares the shit out of me, but it isn't the technology. I'm afraid for my daughter. I want you to bring her home. Whatever it takes, whatever it costs, all I care about is my little girl."

"You need to know our methods aren't always traditional. Forget everything you've seen in the movies. What you have to remember is that we'll get the job done. All I need from you is to know you understand there is a plan in motion for Karas's return. We've been putting it together since her identity was confirmed."

"But you just showed me the picture. How—?"

"I sent Carter a text with the same picture. He identified her and told me we were going forward with the mission. He didn't want to waste time, so I put the guys right on it. I'll be meeting with them soon."

Declan turned to Carter. "How will this affect Karas's safety? I have images running through my head right now of people storming wherever in the hell she is and her getting caught in the fray."

"She's at risk now, Dec. There's no way to know how she's being treated other than this picture. Right now, she looks fine but Vallega is unstable and unpredictable."

"Maybe if we contact him. Offer him money," Declan chimed in.

"If he wanted money, he would have made a demand by now." Carter sensed his brother's concern, but they were wasting time. "Look, this is our best shot. We have one goal, Karas's safe return."

"Promise me something." Declan turned to Falcon, concern weighing his words. "If he's hurt my daughter—"

Sensing where Declan was going, Falcon interrupted him. "If he's hurt your daughter, then I'll personally bring the son of a bitch to you so you can help us serve justice."

Chapter 25

Eliana's tiny mouth opened in a suspended state of terror as the oxygen left her body. Teresa stared at me, helpless in any endeavor to give comfort. I ignored Manny, staring instead at the red handprint as it raised on her cheek in an angry welt. The shaking baby tried to suck in her fill of air. Once she had a fresh supply of wind in her lungs, her pain escaped as she screamed in anguish. Anger splashed from my gut to my throat, nearly drowning me in rage. It burned a molten trail through every cell in my body. Eliana's cry shattered my heart, and what remained were jagged pieces with which I planned to slit Manny's throat. She emptied herself, a rattle of anguish finishing that monumental first wail. Tears poured from her eyes. As my father's daughter, I was familiar with the weeping of children but never had I heard a sound like the one that surged from that little girl. I looked to Teresa, an eerie calm possessing me. "Take the baby."

She reacted instantly, taking Eliana from my arms, cradling her in her own. As Manny paced, lost in his fury, I watched as Teresa took the baby to safety. There were many hiding places in this building, and I had no doubt Teresa would take her far away from Manny's madness—to the safe room.

Once I was satisfied they were a healthy distance away, I turned to Manny. "Are you out of your mind?" The havoc he'd unleashed wracked my sanity into a frenzied ride, and I straddled it ferociously. "Why would you hit a baby?"

"She wouldn't shut up." His matter of fact justification offended me.

"You will never do that again."

"I will do whatever is needed."

"You don't hit a crying child to make them stop crying."

"No, but there *are* ways to make her stop."

"Yes! Comfort!"

"There are other ways. More permanent ways."

The look in Manny's eyes sent a bone-chilling shot down my spine, unnerving me. Something had made him come unhinged, and his comment about "more permanent ways . . ." *Oh my God!*

Somewhere, deep in the recesses of my mind, I knew exactly what he meant, and an undeniable storm erupted at my core. Every cell within me was infused with a depth of hatred I'd never felt before. I couldn't—wouldn't—let him hurt Eliana, but I had to stay calm. I showed nothing. I internalized the feelings, channeling the adrenaline rush inward. I'd need it to take whatever action was necessary to keep Eliana safe.

I'd known the moment Manny's hand connected with the baby's face he was no different than my father—but I was. Every person had their non-negotiable hard limit, and I'd just discovered mine. As a child, I'd watched as wives and girlfriends sat by and tolerated violence against their children. Men with no conscience beat women and hurt little girls. Leading the pack of dogs, my father was one of the worst. I knew about my father's business. He used and bartered women as currency, all while maiming and torturing anyone who opposed him. I had a breaking point—child abuse. Manny's act had earned my hatred and unleashed my vengeance. No matter what I had to do, I would not let Manny hurt Eliana again. I would eliminate the cruel curse my father had cast.

Papi had tried to break all his children with beatings. He'd been successful with my siblings, but I'd been a stubborn girl and refused to cry. His methods of discipline never worked on me, but, one time, he'd pushed me to the edge.

Barely a teenager, I quickly learned my looks permitted me to manipulate men. My body had developed earlier than most girls. My breasts were high, full, and round. I wore no bra and my nipples hardened at the slightest friction. Compared to the other girls, my legs were longer with toned calves and thighs that melded into curvy hips and a tight ass. If I swayed them in just the right manner my father's men, both young and old, noticed. Of course, I accepted their compliments. They were always accompanied by an offer of some sort. "Marianna, can I get you a drink? Marianna, let me carry that for you," etc. I loved the attention. But my father didn't like it at all. He had other plans for me.

One of my father's younger men, Raul, made a comment to me, one that implied he would like his tongue between my thighs. We never suspected my father was within earshot. His justice was swift. The man lost the tongue with which he so graciously offered to lick me, and I received the bitter end of my father's belt.

Never had I received such a ferocious beating. He made me lay over the edge of my bed and yanked my shorts off and then he delivered the lashes. Over and over he beat me. The tender flesh of my back, ass, and legs were whipped with the force of someone possessed. Eventually, I went numb from pain, a possibility I didn't know existed until that day, escaping to a safe place inside of my own head. When he finally stopped neither of us moved. I could hear him panting from the exertion of his efforts. My eyes burned with unshed tears, but I did not cry—and I was damned proud that I didn't.

I released the gripped bed linens, splaying my fingers wide, and then pushed myself up to a standing position. I pulled up my shorts, the friction of the denim material like sandpaper on a sunburn, I tried not to wince. I turned to my father and looked him straight in the eye. I was proud, defiant, and so much better than him. He wanted my tears, and I denied him. So, he backhanded me in the face. Just as Manny did to poor Eliana.

I thought I'd won with my father, but I should never have shown my hand. I should have cried and let him think he'd won. Maybe then he would have stopped, by my firmly held insolence further incited his anger.

When Papi left the room, I bent over, hugging myself at the waist. It was a short-lived respite. I heard a scream. My innocent twin sister was intercepted as she was walking in the hallway. I stuck my head out the bedroom door in time to see my father dragging her into our room.

Papi held Marchelle by her hair, his arm so high it made her stand on tiptoe. "You see this, Marianna?" He jerked her back and forth like a ragdoll. "She might look like you, but I'll make damn sure she doesn't become the slut that you are!"

He beat my sister, not as ferociously as he did me, but he gave her a sound whipping and he made me watch. I bit the inside of my cheeks until the coppery taste of blood filled the inside of my mouth. It wasn't until later that I learned why he quit hitting Marchelle after several strokes; she was his chattel. A commodity to strike a bargain with a rival cartel. He was planning to marry her off to the cartel leader's son. Marchelle was disposable to my father, but bargaining a treaty with damaged merchandise wouldn't do.

He was a monster who relished the infliction of pain.

As I held my sobbing sister, I examined my conscience. Surely if there were a God, he would forgive me for ridding the earth of a devil.

That night, as my father lay drunk and sleeping, I held a pillow over his face while he took his last breath. I had no regrets after killing him—and I would have no regrets for killing my husband.

"You have no idea the clusterfuck you've created, Marianna."

My spine stiffened, a steel-like resolve making it ramrod straight, and just like that night with my father, I looked the devil in the eye. "Hurt Eliana again, and I'll kill you."

Chapter 26

Manny closed the distance between us and caged me against the wall. "You would dare put that child before me? I should have known. You knew who she was, didn't you? That's why you wanted her."

Flecks of spittle hit my face as he spat out the words like a madman. I had no idea what he was ranting about, but I knew I wouldn't show fear. If Manny snapped, nothing I could say or do would make a difference. All my distress would do was incite his anger further.

I didn't understand it, this feeling I had for the baby, but for the first time in my life, I didn't care about myself. I cared for Eliana—maybe even loved her—and I wouldn't allow her to be another child sacrifice of the cartel. Too much innocent blood had been spilled already.

"Answer me!" Manny wrapped his hand around my throat, pinning me in.

I seethed the words through gritted teeth. "I don't know what you're talking about."

"Liar!" He shouted. "Fuck!" He banged a heavy fist beside me and then pushed away. His war was with himself. Once again, his nervous habit took hold and he relentlessly walked in circles. "I've given you everything you ever wanted. I've saved you more times than I can count. You have no idea the things I've done for you, Marianna. When your father wanted to hurt you, I goaded him into using me as your whipping boy." He continued with a maniacal laugh as he threw his hands up and talked into the air. "Oh, you should have heard the details of how he planned to rid himself of you. His fiercest competitor wanted you, and for years your father refused, but then you grew up, and your father saw a savvy business deal in the making."

"But he died first. I took care of my father." My tone was calm. I thought Manny would be surprised at my revelation and my mind raced. I could kill my husband just as easily, and a thousand different ways to do so danced in my head.

"You?" He stopped moving and turned his attention to me. "You took care of your father?" Laughter sprang from his chest. "And just how did you do that? Please. Humor me. I want to know."

I stood my ground, refusing to answer. Manny

flopped into the rocker, his stature much too big for the piece. He pointed an angry finger at me.

"You didn't do shit, Marianna. Let me tell you what really happened that night." He kicked the ottoman out in my direction. "Sit. I think you'll like this story."

I didn't move and it angered him.

"SIT DOWN, MARIANNA!"

The booming command bounced off the walls. Though fear rattled uneasiness in my knees, I forced them steady. It was only a few steps from where I was standing to where Manny demanded I sit. I kept my chin high as I stayed the course and took a seat, my posture the envy of any Catholic schoolgirl. Manny turned away to collect his thoughts. I reached into my pocket for my phone, quickly hitting the function for voice recordings, and stuffed it back into my pocket. Even if he killed me, someone would find my phone and play it back. *God help me!*

Manny turned back in my direction, a smile on his lips. He looked like a man who'd lost his mind. "Such a good girl you were that night. Your father beat you, and then he beat your sister. Marchelle couldn't take a beating like you, Marianna. She never could." He got lost in his thoughts for a moment, then looked up at me with sad eyes. "I wish I could have helped you, but if I had, he would have killed me."

I managed my breaths, regulating my respiration to a more calm and even pace. I had no idea what revelations Manny had. I didn't know he'd been there that night.

"Carlos was exhausted. He went downstairs into his office. I followed him." He looked away from me, staring into nothingness as he recalled the night from long ago. "I waited for him to sit in his big, black leather chair. Once he did, I knocked on the door . . .

You look like you need a drink, Papi. Rough night?"

"Bitches. It's always bitches." His voice was thick, and his tone was grave. I walked over to the bar.

"A double?" I asked though I knew he always drank more.

"A double, double tonight, Manny. I have too much on my mind and need to sleep."

I knew he would sleep, but I had planned a more permanent one. I put poison in his drink, just enough to make him groggy. They were his own pills, just more of them. I'd used the muddler from the bar earlier in the day and had hidden the powder once I'd crushed the tablets. It took about twenty minutes.

"I'm going to bed." He stood up, losing his balance.

"You need help?" I offered.

He waved me off, dismissing me without a word. I followed him, lagging behind so he wouldn't see me. I knew that in about another half hour he would be passed out. That was when I planned to kill him."

Manny looked at me. "I see the surprise in your eyes, Marianna. You didn't think I would let him get away with it, did you? He had plans for all of his daughters, but your fate . . . well, let's just say your future was entrusted to a man whose nickname was *el Carnicero*. The man liked to cut up little girls."

I'd slipped out of my shoes and bent over to leave them near the stairs. I planned to move into your father's room and finish him. Imagine my surprise when I watched little Marisol slip inside before I could.

As soon as you went in, I followed. You were so intent on your task of smothering your father you never noticed I was there. I opened the door just a crack, and I watched as you straddled your father's belly and rode him as he resisted death. I was so proud of you that night. My ángel vengador. You thought you killed him. I waited until you returned to your room and went in to inspect your work. That was when I saw him breathe— heard him, actually. He took a breath that was a snore. Maybe it was sleep apnea. Who knows? The pillow was near his head, so I finished the job for you.

Rousing from his recollection, he leaned forward and placed his hands on my knees. "So, you see, Marianna, I would do anything to protect you, and, now, in order to do that, I have to get rid of that baby."

Tremors rocked my insides, spiking my heart rate. The tightly reined emotions I had only moments ago successfully kept in checked exploded. "You can't do that. She's mine!"

His smile turned sinister, his eyes beady and soulless as his words scraped at what was left of my composure, as he revealed a truth that rocked me to my core.

"No. She's Declan's."

Chapter 27

I was in shock. *Declan's child?*

"Surprised? So was I. Apparently, I should have just bought a child. Instead I chose proper channels. Seems the *proper channels* have dirty deals, too. I don't know all of the details yet, but I will find out. The adoption agency screwed us both, Marianna. What they didn't count on was my ability to make the problem go away."

The horrifying, sick smile on Manny's face was like none I'd seen before, and the tension in the room thickened so that I could barely breathe. Hot reality burned bright as I realized what Manny had done, and I feared I might pass out. My stomach cramped, and I feared I might vomit. How could he have done this? How could Manny have been so stupid? How could I have been so stupid? I'd trusted him to handle all of the paperwork, except that he knew there was none. Was he crazy?

Declan's child? Didn't he realize we both could go to jail for the rest of our lives?

Just as I was about to unleash a litany of questions, Manny's cell phone rang. He pulled it from his pocket and looked at it. Sheer disgust chewed up his expression. He hit the screen with his finger to connect the call and then put the phone on speaker.

"I'm in the middle of something. I can't talk."

"We have a problem, Manny. We need to talk." The deep timbre of my uncle's voice came through the phone.

Peeved at the nuisance, Manny's face went tight. His teeth clenched, his eyes narrowed, and he rolled his neck from side to side. He looked as if he were getting ready for a physical fight. "Now isn't a good time, César."

"Then make it a good time. Someone has breached security." My uncle's tone was firm and demanding, and the resulting scowl on Manny's face revealed he didn't like being ordered around by an underling.

"You're the head of security. Handle it." His response was smart and clipped.

César's tone became just the opposite, nonchalant almost. "If you care about your image, I think you might want to see this. Your rebuke of Kate Frampton and ADDEX didn't sit well, apparently. She's made a statement. Your name was mentioned several times."

"God damn it!" Manny's arm flew down while still holding the phone. I was no longer the object of his attention as he stared past me to gather his thoughts. After a moment, he lifted the phone back up to speak into it. "Where?"

"My house. I'm in the monitoring room."

"I'll be there soon." Manny disconnected the call and gave me a threatening look. "I won't be long. Don't you dare go anywhere, Marianna. We'll finish this little talk when I get back."

I barely breathed as Manny adjusted his clothes. Without a word he left the room, slamming the door on his way out.

I wasted no time once he was gone, running through the dressing room, into the bathroom. It seemed an eternity before I entered the panic room.

"Is she okay?" The question rushed out, riding a wave of concern. Teresa assured me that all was well with a simple nod. Only she, Eliana, and a member of my security team were in there. As I looked at Eliana sorrow washed over me. Her cheek was already developing bruising, dark shades starting to emerge. Red-rimmed from crying, her eyes were an even more pronounced shade of blue. She looked so tired. Broken. Hurt. She was still sniffling as her head lay on Teresa's shoulder. *That son of a bitch!*

I looked over to the man at the desk. "Was all of that recorded?"

"Sí." He had a sad look in his eyes. "I'm sorry. He should never have done that."

Though his sentiment was appreciated, there was

little time to spare. If we were to get Eliana to safety, we had to do it while Manny was gone.

"Gracias. I need you to do something for me. Call the other three on the team. Tell them I need help getting out of the country."

He nodded and proceeded to do as I asked. I turned to Teresa. "We have to get her out of here." She nodded. "Pack the diaper bag and bring the Benadryl. It will be better for all of us if Eliana sleeps through this."

Teresa handed me the baby. She was worn out and slumped against my chest, her head tucked against my neck, and I placed my chin on her head. *Sweet baby girl.*

Of all the scenarios I'd run through my head when Manny first proposed adoption, I would never, ever have thought he would kidnap Declan's child. I wouldn't have even entertained the idea. It was ludicrous to take a child with such a high-profile parent. At one time in my life I wanted to get back at Declan and his crew for the trouble they'd caused me. I would have stopped at nothing to destroy them, but not now. I don't know if it was the medication prescribed for the bipolar disorder. I didn't know when or why I'd developed a conscience. What I did know was that I had boundaries, and my boundaries extended to adults. That whole group deserved every hurt I could inflict. They caused me so much pain, and I gave them back an equal portion, but they were adults. I could never hurt Eliana. I wasn't that much of a monster. I loved that little girl. *Wait! What?* Oh my God. I loved her. How did this happen? *Don't be naïve, Marianna. You know how.*

It was his well-orchestrated plan. When we'd returned from the US, Manny had insisted we polish up our images. He wanted us to make them squeaky clean so he would become a favorite in the political arena. Adopting a child was part of the strategy. A means to an end. But this? He had to have known that nothing good could come from kidnapping Declan's daughter. I could have understood it if he acquired a child through the cartel. Some poor trafficked baby that he thought would fit his prerequisites. This was a disaster. No matter how hard he could ever have tried to spin this story in our favor, it would never have worked. *And now he wanted Eliana dead.*

Though I was raised in this environment, I would never fully understand the cartels' methods. Of course, I'd turned a blind eye to some, and others I'd manipulated myself. There were even more that I'd become desensitized to, but there were some I'd never accept.

I was an intelligent girl and, in my teens, had come to realize that drugs and whores weren't their only sources of income. I'd overheard my father talking about the sale of people, that it commanded a great deal of money. That was when I realized my sweet little friend, Eliana, had been sold. It had been years since I'd seen her walk down the hallway to her fate, and now that I knew what that was, it sickened me.

My childhood Eliana must have commanded a higher price with her blonde hair and blue eyes. If ever I could have loved someone, it was her. Children have no concept of time, but I remembered Eliana living with us long enough for us to have formed a bond. My heart hurt just thinking of her. It was a pain I'd locked away. Manny had opened that door when he slapped the baby. Declan's child or not, I would never forgive him.

The fear that had settled in the pit of my stomach when Manny had hit the baby was now a chasm. As I snuggled Eliana, I now knew our time together was short.

I couldn't get the memory my childhood Eliana being led down the hall by that horrid man out of my head. I remembered his clothing, but I couldn't remember his identity. My eyes were fixed on Eliana as she left me, and when I closed my eyes, I could still see her. The pain in her expression equaled mine. But I was a child then and had no way to save her. I held baby Eliana closer to me as I tried to make sense of what had transpired.

Manny's revelation of the baby's true identity filled me with questions. It was rare that we watched television, and especially American channels because Manny abhorred the shows. He did, however, keep up with world events and I would have thought that a kidnapping of a child with a parent as prominent as Declan Sinclair would have made international news. I hadn't looked at a newspaper since Eliana had arrived. Instead, I'd stayed in my own little world.

In the beginning, I'd watched Teresa with Eliana because Manny had insisted I do so. He'd wanted me to bond with the child, though I knew that would never happen, I didn't want any upset in my life. I enjoyed the immense respect and adoration I received from the people of Colombia. Manny was a political favorite, and the inclusion I received as a byproduct was something I craved. The elite loved me simply because of my position as his wife.

At Manny's insistence, I reluctantly went to the nursery every day at my assigned time to acclimate myself to motherhood. At first, I felt inconvenienced. I resisted any feelings. Something happened when I saw Eliana with Teresa. She was infectious with her joyful belly laughs. I began to feel happiness. I couldn't pinpoint the exact moment when the emotion arrived, but I felt something for this baby—and I was the only one who could save her.

The pain that Declan must be going through. The thought was sobering, proving that my mindset had most definitely changed—but not so much that I wanted to give Eliana back.

I wanted alternatives to keep the baby with me, selfish bitch that I was. I didn't care if Declan and Aria ever got their baby back. They could have others. *Couldn't they?*

The realization I would soon be suffering the same fate that they'd suffered was like a sucker punch. Once I returned her, I would never see Eliana again. Though, initially adamant that I did not want a child, this little one's sweetness won me over. She was a delight, really. Like my childhood Eliana, she only offered herself. The gifts of smiles and laughter, and she gave those freely. I would never see them again. *Unless I took her away somewhere with me.*

A war erupted on the battlefield of my mind. She was already missing. I could provide for her the same as Declan, maybe even better. I could escape with her to a private island. Raise her in my image. I entertained the thought because the prospect of never holding Eliana again grieved me. The selfish voice inside my head screamed at me to take her away, yet somewhere, perhaps in the contents of a medication bottle, I'd developed a conscience, and it was screaming equally as loud. My heart ached, and my stomach twisted as I thought of never seeing my baby again—and she was mine. Manny had given her to me. *But she'll never really be yours.*

I squashed the thought. I don't need to follow anyone's rules. I knew who I was: Marisol Franzi, super bitch. I took what I wanted. I didn't ask permission! I could have anything I wanted. Money was no object. *But this baby isn't for sale.*

I closed my eyes and did something rare; I connected with my heart. It was in pain and it was terrified. I didn't know what to do with the foreign feelings. My mind spun under the weight of the decision before me. My insides shook, making me feel nauseous. I asked myself if all of this was worth it. Could I let Manny dispose of her and get another child, or could I take her to her father and face the law? Either way I knew I would never see her again.

Chapter 28

M anny

"WHAT'S so important that you needed to pull me away from my wife?" Irritation chewed at Manny's disposition, the words exposing him.

"Why don't you sit down?" César's brow quirked as a smile played at his lips. He tipped his chin in the direction Manny had entered. A huge, expressionless man in a black tee shirt closed the door. Manny was big, but this man was bigger. The material strained tightly around his biceps and equally across his chest. The holster was snug on the man's thigh, his gun accessible within a few seconds. He closed the door and then stood guard in front of it.

César repeated the same beckoning motion to

another man, equally as large and identically armed. "Get Sr. Vallega a drink, would you please?" That man, also, did César's bidding. These two didn't seem familiar, making Manny uncomfortable. He thought he knew everyone in security.

The man handed a drink to Manny and then he, too, went to guard the door. None of these actions went without notice. He took a seat, drink in hand, and turned his attention to César.

"What's going on?" The words scraped through his teeth, but he had calmed his tone down from his earlier comment. His gut told him that something was amiss and these two had been given instructions that might not be in his best interest.

"You might want to drink that down before I show you."

Manny never took his eyes off the older man. He drank the scotch in one gulp and noted that César was watching him just as carefully. He took the glass from his lips and held it out to show that it was empty. "Get to the point."

Though there were several chairs in the technology room, César dragged one over until it was beside Manny's. César reached into his pocket, crossed his legs, and sat back to watch. He pulled out a remote control and pushed a button. A partition on the wall separated to reveal a very large monitor. He pressed another button, and the lights grew dim. Yet another and a video of a press conference began to play. *Kate! What the hell?*

"Thank you all for coming today. ADDEX Pharmaceuticals is dedicated to meeting the needs of patients all over the world. Our research and development are comprised of the latest technology and the most intelligent scientific minds. This combination has placed our company at the forefront when addressing the needs of those individuals who suffer and need prescription drugs. We were the first to develop medicines that treat the areas of diabetes, Alzheimer's, AIDs, and others. We were the first company to offer various drugs to combat mental illness. We provide cutting edge technology to the modern world. Today is no exception. We, at ADDEX, are proud to announce that the FDA has just approved another drug to combat drug overdoses. In laymen's terms, it blocks the effects of opioid overdose.

"This new drug is more powerful and more effective than the current market drug of our competitor. We are proud to unveil the drug StOVER.

"StOVER is a quick acting drug with little to no side effects. This drug will be available for distribution in the United States within the next six months, and, if all goes well, we're hoping to release it internationally by the end of the year.

"ADDEX would like to thank Mr. César Josef for his generosity. As you know, Mr. Josef's home country, Colombia, is inundated with drug-related social issues, and Mr. Josef is dedicated to eradicating illegal drug use and the collateral damage from the same. He has been a generous benefactor to ADDEX, helping to further our goals toward bringing this drug to the market in an expeditious manner. ADDEX will, with the help of leaders like Mr. Josef, get this drug and others to those who need it. We would like to say, publicly, that we appreciate his support.

"As a side note, I have just learned that Mr. Josef is throwing his hat into the political ring and will be running for the honored position of President of Colombia. We wish him all the very best."

The blood drained from Manny's face as he watched Kate gather her papers from the podium, tap them into order, and turn to walk away. Reporters started shouting questions, but one was loud and clear. She paused.

Reporter: "Ms. Frampton, is there any truth to the rumor that ADDEX Pharmaceuticals and Manuel Vallega were working on the very project that you just mentioned? What changed so that Mr. Vallega is out?"

K. Frampton (smiling sweetly): "Though we weren't prepared to entertain questions, I'll answer this one to clear up any misunderstandings; whatever you heard, it was a rumor, and you've been misinformed. ADDEX is dedicated to the legal distribution of drugs. We have it on competent authority that Mr. Vallega is on the opposing side of our mission. Thank you."

The screen showed more reporters clamoring for

attention. Kate ignored them as she walked away. In the crowd behind her was Senator Ford. He was glad for the low lighting in the room so no one could see his reaction, but the light also had a downside; it limited Manny's ability to see César.

Engrossed in what he was watching, he didn't see César get out of his chair. He was now beside him, resting his hand on Manny's shoulder. Manny jerked it away and rose slowly from his own chair. He waited until he'd reached his full height, which was several inches taller than Marianna's uncle. Looking down, he met César's eyes. "I'll give you an hour head start to get out of the country, and then I'm going to send my men to hunt you like the dog you are."

A smirk hooked the corner of César's lips. "Your men? I think you mean my men."

"Carlos handpicked me. He groomed me to take over. Everyone knows that. Even you."

"Yes, but not everyone likes it." César crossed his arms, eyeing Manny with sick amusement. "I'll tell you what, I'll give you what you so graciously offered me; you have that same hour to gather Marianna and get out of the country." Turning his back on Manny, he paused as a thought occurred to him. He peered over his shoulder. "I will give you a piece of advice; take that baby with you. You looked the proverbial gift horse in the mouth, and it bit you in the ass."

"What are you talking about?" Manny demanded.

César turned, amusement dancing in his eyes. "Oh,

you didn't know? Kate arranged it. She knew how badly you wanted a child. She knew of one that was available. The agency who had procured the child had an affiliation with ADDEX. They were wondering what to do with the child when Kate told them of your desire to build a family. I told her I thought that it was a splendid idea to direct the little one to you and Marianna. I thought she told you, but then, she's not one to brag about gifts."

César left the room through another door, and the two bodyguards opened wide the ones at Manny's back. He refused to show humiliation in front of these goons and remained composed. He straightened his jacket as he exited the room, never breaking stride until he was outside the house. Miguel was waiting for him in the car, and Manny threw himself inside.

"Do you know who in the organization is loyal to me and not to César or the cartel? Only to me." Miguel nodded. "Good. I need you to assemble them while I get Marianna. Call the airport to get the jet ready. We're taking a trip."

Manny mentally ticked off a list of potential problems. *That conniving bastard!* César could have already sent men to secure the jet and prevent Marianna and him from leaving. If that proved to be the case, there was always the car. They would have to take off roads to get out of the country. They might be able to make it to Panama or Costa Rica by car, Mexico City by plane.

Money! They needed money. He would empty the

safes and take what was there. There were two, one in the bedroom and one in his office. Between them was at least a few hundred thousand. It would be enough for now until he accessed his private, offshore accounts. They would make it. He could keep his head about him in the worst circumstances.

Forming a quick plan, he could think of only one problem. "And, Miguel, find Teresa and that baby and bring them both down to the dungeon."

Chapter 29

A ria

DECLAN WALKED into his brother's office ahead of me. It was almost go time. The team had several locations and was gathering some equipment from this one, but then were off to another location to solidify mission logistics and collect the necessary paraphernalia for the rescue. Carter wasn't part of the team, but Declan told me he had every faith in Falcon, Marcus, and their team.

"What are you doing here?" Carter was surprised to see us. I'm sure he thought Declan and I would be better off at his house while they all waited for news.

"Did you really think I was going to let these guys go after my daughter without me seeing what they look like? Not a chance in hell. Karas isn't an asset, she's my little girl."

Before Carter could argue the point with his brother, I stepped out from behind him. If the situation weren't so grave, I would have laughed at his reaction. One brow quirked as a grimacing smile lifted the corners of his lips. "Seriously? You, too?"

I answered in a heartbeat. "Yes, really. I want to look these men in the eye, remember their faces. It is important to me to know the people who are putting their lives on the line to save my baby."

Carter looked at us both, studying our expressions. The anxiety we felt on the inside was sure to be mirrored on our faces. I wasn't sure if he would let us pass by him. His body language said, "no trespassing," but there was a war in his eyes. He stood with his legs apart, and his arms folded tightly across his chest. I locked eyes with him, begging him to grant us this one, small favor. I knew this was breaking whatever protocol they had and that no one else would have been able to get past my brother-in-law, but we weren't just anybody—and neither was Karas.

"Oh, for God's sake." The comment was said under his breath as he rolled his eyes up toward the heavens. Then he looked from me to Declan, shaking his head in disbelief that he would break his own rules. He might have been able to keep Declan at bay, and I didn't care if they spent all afternoon arguing the point after the fact, but there was no way I was leaving without achieving my goal. "C'mon." Resignation replaced his former determination, and Carter turned, motioning for us to follow him.

This was the first time I'd been to the new offices. When I walked in, I thought it looked like any other business, but Carter led us to the back. Declan watched me, noting the surprise in my eyes as the elevator went down. When Carter opened the door for us, my eyes widened further.

"Wow . . ." My voice trailed away under the weight of shock as I looked left to right, then up and down. "This is, like, crazy."

Carter smiled, as did Falcon as he approached us. "All of this—and what the guys have in their other location—are what's going to bring Karas home to you." Karas home. The thought brought stinging tears to my eyes. Falcon noticed and placed his hand on my shoulder, stooping down to look me in the eye. "She's in good hands, Aria. Promise."

I looked over at the group of men. For the most part, they ignored me as they put on their gear. We'd parked in the back of the building, and when we had, we saw two black Hummers on the lot. They had to be transportation for these men. I couldn't see how all of them would fit in a regular car. They were all brawn and muscle and looked as fierce as tanks. I had no doubt they would ride roughshod over anyone and anything that got in the way of their mission. I looked at Falcon.

"Would you introduce me to them, please?" The plea in my voice neared desperation. Falcon looked at Carter, who nodded in approval.

"Sure." Falcon motioned for me to go ahead of him. He captured everyone's attention as he called out to them. "Hey, guys. A minute, please."

Each paused, suspending their individual tasks for a moment. Falcon, standing behind me, placed a hand on my shoulder. "This is Aria Sinclair. Karas's mom."

Some tipped their chins to acknowledge me, and I heard a few say "ma'am." I walked over to the first one. Declan followed behind.

The man was well over six feet—about six feet five inches, I'd say. The look in his green eyes was sincere. I noted a scar from the corner of his right eye that went up into his short, brown hair. "Digger Jones, ma'am." I nodded and then turned my attention to the next man. He wasn't as tall as Digger. His thick, silver hair and the lines etched on his face said he was older than the other men. His eyes were so blue they reminded me of Karas's.

I swallowed the lump in my throat as he held his hand out for me to shake. "Ace Robertson."

"Your eyes remind me of my daughter's, Mr. Robertson."

"It's Ace, ma'am. And, hopefully, soon you'll be looking at hers instead of these old eyes."

The next two men approached. "Lee Forest,

ma'am, and this here's Henry Ford." I looked at the second man, surprise in my eyes.

"No, ma'am. No relation," Mr. Ford said in a voice that sounded like a mix of gravel and whiskey. He gave me a half smile as his eyes twinkled. "Our last name is Ford, and I was conceived in the back of a Ford pickup. My ma and pa thought Henry was a good name."

Lee pointed over to a horseshoe-shaped desk. Large screen monitors filled every space of the wall above it, and a great amount of technical equipment sat on top of the desk as well as around it. "That there is Mike Harris, best IT guy in the business. We call him 'Mustang Sally' because that's all he drives."

Mr. Harris kept his face in the monitors but raised a hand in greeting. That wouldn't do for me, so I walked over to him. As I approached his shoulder, I saw that he had a child-size sand bucket filled with Ferraro Rocher hazelnut candies on his desk. I pointed to them. "I like them, too." He looked up at me, his brown eyes the same color as his hair.

"You can have some if you want," he said as he held them out to me.

I tipped my chin in the direction of the equipment. "Is all of this stuff going to help you find my daughter? It looks very state of the art."

His expression was reassuring as he smiled and nodded. "If you think this is something, you should see my real stuff. This is just satellite necessities that I have at every location."

I gave him a satisfied smile and when I turned away from him I saw all of the men's eyes on me. "I'll be praying for your safety—and my daughter's."

I wanted to say more, something inspirational perhaps, but I couldn't. I could barely speak, the few words I had said nearly caught in my throat. The magnitude of what was at stake weighed heavily in my heart. These men were putting their lives at risk going after Manny and Marisol, but they were our daughter's best chance of coming home.

Chapter 30

The only belongings Teresa and I were taking was a full diaper bag for Eliana and our purses. In each of them was one of the disposable phones I'd purchased in Vegas. I was so glad I hadn't thrown them away. I'd locked the three of us in with Roberto in the panic room. Having previously instructed him of my plan to get out of the country, I looked over at the man who'd witnessed it all. All of this had taken less than half an hour, but time was of the essence. I had no idea how long Manny would be with Tío César.

Teresa held a sleeping Eliana. "Were you able to get us on a flight, Berto?" He nodded. Both my phone and Teresa's pinged as Roberto handed me the portfolios.

"Here are your passports. I just sent the boarding passes to your phones. I also hacked into the system to get you priority boarding."

"Thank you. Please tell me you have everything that happened in that room recorded. Manny hurting the baby and his admitting she's Declan's?" He nodded. "Good." I grabbed a notepad and pen from his desk and started writing. "I want you to send a flash drive with a copy of that entire incident to this address." I tore off the sheet of paper and handed it to him. This was my only hope to prove my innocence. If Manny was going to go to jail for kidnapping, I wasn't going with him.

"Yes, ma'am."

"Thank you." Though he was only doing his job, he was also trying to cover our tracks. Teresa and I were racing against the clock to get the baby out of Colombia without Manny's notice. If he found us, I had no doubt he would kill all of us.

"Ma'am?" He held out his palm. It contained a set of keys. "These are the keys to my car. Sr. Vallega would never think you'd be driving something other than your own. It's a black Dodge Journey, and it's parked near the east entrance to the house. I'll follow you on my monitors and simultaneously hack into the house security every step of the way. No one in main security will see you leaving."

I nodded. I'd vetted the security team for the baby well, but it was obvious this man's dislike for Manny ran deep. His loyalty to me and to Eliana's welfare might be the only thing that would save us. "Thank you, Berto. For everything."

We exited the panic room, and I looked over at Teresa. She held Eliana in her arms. "Ready?" I asked.

"Sí." We both spoke in low tones, terrified we might give ourselves away. She adjusted Eliana in her arms. The baby's head was on her shoulder and Teresa had her open hand on her back to steady her.

I peeked outside the nursery door and looked to the left and right. There was no one in sight. I looked at Teresa behind me. "Let's go." Slinging the diaper bag onto my shoulder, I moved forward with Teresa following closely behind me. I pressed the button for the elevator, and it opened immediately. Thankfully, where it would land on the ground floor was only steps away from the east entrance of the building.

Just as the elevator came to a stop, Eliana became restless. The door opened the same time as Eliana's mouth. Teresa and I looked at her, horrified she might let out a cry—but she didn't. Her head slumped down on Teresa's shoulder, and we both let out a sigh of relief. I checked outside the open elevator door to see if anyone would spot us. Once satisfied there was no one there, I turned. Looking over my shoulder, I motioned with my head for Teresa to follow me. We approached the door to the outside lot. It was commonly referred to as the delivery entrance, but it was where Manny had all of his men park their cars before coming into the house. I had just barely opened it when I saw one of Manny's men in the parking lot. *Shit!*

I quickly and quietly closed the door. Placing my

finger to my lips, I looked at Teresa. The door had beveled glass near the top. Although not a clear view, I could still peek out and see well enough to know the man was smoking a cigarette.

One drag. Two drags. Three drags. I watched the exhaled smoke as it dissipated into the air, wondering if my plan to get Eliana back to Declan would go up in smoke just as easily.

Finally, he dropped the cigarette on the ground, stamped it out, and got into his car. Another few minutes and I watched him drive away. "C'mon," I whispered to Teresa.

She followed behind me. I looked down at the key fob and hit the unlock button. The headlights flashed to indicate which car that it was. We rushed over to it, and I opened the back, driver's side door. "Get in and stay low. If Manny's going to look for us, he's going to have them looking for two women and a baby, not one lone woman."

She nodded, acknowledging my directive, and laid the baby down. My heart squeezed inside of my chest as I looked at Eliana's angelic face. Hopefully, she wouldn't remember any of this. *And she'll never remember you.*

Teresa bent over and placed a light blanket over the baby's face to shield her from the lights. Then she lightly laid her own head on top of the baby's stomach and placed her arm protectively around her.

I closed the door quietly, listening for the click of

the latch. Once it was secure, I got into the front seat, started the car, and put it in reverse. I absorbed everything I looked at, quickly determining what I thought could impede our attempt to escape Manny and his plans.

My foot shook from nervousness, and my driving skills were rusty. I hadn't driven a car since arriving in New York all those years ago. After a few minutes going from gas to brake, I finally got the hang of it and I took off toward the gated exit. I thought Roberto might have been able to control them, but my hopes were dashed when we approached. There were two men with guns waiting for us. *Shit! Shit! Shit!*

I stopped, calmly rolling down the window and putting on my best resting bitch face. I feared that, at any moment we would be hauled out of the car and turned over to Manny. I took a deep breath as a man approached and I could feel the perspiration rolling down my back. He had a sinister look on his face. There was no other way out.

"Hello, Sra. Vallega," he greeted me. He looked over at the other guard, who was busy smoking a cigarette and looked to be drunk. He stumbled, and I gave the man at the window a puzzled look. He nodded toward the other man. "Berto called me. I put something in that guy's cigarette. Looks like it's working." He wore a sly smile. "Go ahead. You're all clear."

Relief washed over me as the gates opened in front of us. *Thank God for Roberto!* I wasted no time, speeding up to get through the gates and off the property. "Hold on."

Confident Teresa would keep Eliana from sliding off the seat, I sped away from the estate. Fear crawled up my spine and clouded my thinking. There were so many things that could still go wrong.

Chapter 31

R oberto

FROM THE SAFETY of the panic room, Roberto watched as Manny entered the house. It was apparent his destination was the nursery.

"Marianna!" His voice bellowed through the house and reverberated off the walls. The rage in his tone was unmistakable. He went into the central nursery and looked left and right, and then went into the dressing room. Roberto grinned, realizing that only two doors separated them, but Manny didn't know that. He looked at his monitor, thankful Sra. Vallega hadn't grabbed many clothes for the little one. Not that Manny would have noticed, but nothing appeared out of place.

Fury clouded Manny's expression as a dark crimson color shaded his face and neck. "MARIANNA!" he screamed. He waited for a response, any sign from his wife, but none came.

A storm brewed inside of him, birthing a frenzy of anger. It consumed him, saturating his mind with thoughts of fury and destruction. "FUCK!" Manny reached up to the delicately painted white dowels that held hundreds of tiny outfits. He violently grabbed two handfuls, ripping the fragile clothing from the rack. Manny flung them to the floor and reached for two more, and when he was done, he reached for two more, and after that two more until nothing remained in the closet. He was a portrait of pandemonium, moving past the clothing on the floor toward something else—the shoes.

Manny feverishly pelted walls, figurines, and anything else that decorated the room, with incredible force. Blue shoes, red, white, all were gone from the racks, sacrificed to the havoc he created.

For nearly forty-five minutes Roberto watched from his observation deck, the smirk on his face giving away how he delighted in seeing the bastard fall apart. Berto hated Manny. If he knew he wouldn't risk losing his own life he'd go out there, confront Manny, and murder the bastard. Vallega was responsible for his half brother's death, though Manny didn't know or care about the connection between the two men.

They had the same mother, but different fathers. Their family was close, and his brother was not only blood but his friend. He died by Manny's hand. Berto's brother, Mateo, was one of two men sent to watch over Marianna when she lived in New York. When he came back to Colombia and reported news to Manny that displeased him, he killed him.

That day, Roberto vowed vengeance in his heart. He didn't blame Marianna for wanting to get away from here to have a life of her own, but his brother would never breathe again. He could only hope Marianna would continue to, and he was proud he'd helped her to escape. It was poetic justice, and from the panic room, Roberto had an ideal front-row seat.

Roberto watched Manny, bent over at the waist, in the middle of a pile of destroyed baby items, breathing heavily from the exertion. It took him a few moments to compose himself. When he stood, he pulled the cell out of his pocket. He jabbed one number.

"Where the fuck is Marianna? Who's watching her?"

Roberto watched and listened. It was apparent to Roberto that Manny was calling the security room. They would find nothing. Berto had jammed their monitors with Marianna's every step to escape, all the while replacing the security surveillance with his own footage.

"Did she leave the house?"

By the look on Manny's face, it was apparent he was dissatisfied with the answer. "God damn it! Get the men and meet me in the den. I want her found, even if we have to search every inch of this house. She's got to be here somewhere."

At Manny's direction, the occupants of the house were in an uproar. Roberto watched as the entire security team went room to room looking for someone they would never find. Satisfaction filled him. Like effervescent bubbles, he saw the beauty in watching a smug, self-righteous bastard like Manny fall apart, piece by piece. He didn't care about the other men, nor did he care about being discovered. He'd helped Sra. Vallega design this room. His own mother would have been safe in here, bless her dearly departed soul. *This is for you, Mami.*

As he switched the views on the monitors to keep tabs on the men, the one he focused on was Manny. In every room, he checked under beds, inside of closets, and behind curtains. For more than an hour they scoured every corner, and with every room they found empty, Manny's anger escalated. Silently, Roberto hoped the man would drop dead, but then that would be too peaceful. Manny deserved to die in one of the many violent manners he inflicted death on others—with torture.

Manny gathered all the men in the hallway of the last room they checked. "Nothing?" He looked into their faces as a chorus of "no's" played in different keys of baritone.

Confused, Manny stared at the floor and then subconsciously fell into his habit of walking in circles while deep in thought. He said nothing for the first few minutes, and then his head snapped up. "She's gone to him," he said to himself. He then looked at the men. "She's gone to the States!" He punched the wall with such ferocity that either his knuckles or the wall should have cracked.

Once recovered, he straightened his shoulders and turned to the first man behind him. "Call Santiago. Tell him I want the plane ready to go in thirty minutes." The man immediately pulled out his cell to make the call. He pointed to another man. "You! Get the car." He hustled down the hallway. "And, you!" he pointed to a third man. "I want weapons. I don't know what I'll run into, but I want to be prepared." He, too, took off jogging down the hallway. "I need a few men to go with me. Declan Sinclair could be in several different places. I want to cover them all."

It looked like a pep talk before a sporting event. Testosterone simmering as the men pumped themselves up for a fight. "I'll tell you where to go. If you find Marianna before I do, do not—I repeat, do not—touch her. I'll take care of her myself."

"What about the nanny and the baby?" one of the men asked.

Manny's expression shifted from stoic concentration to dark violence. Disgust curled his lip, and his jaw moved back and forth as he ground his teeth. He looked at the man who'd posed the question, a thirst for blood in his eyes. "Kill them."

Chapter 32

I pulled up to the airport drop off point for our airline, suddenly realizing I couldn't leave the car there without raising the suspicion of airport security. We didn't have time for another option, and I was unfamiliar with all the security rules. Up until this moment I'd always had the luxury of either having the convenience of a private jet or someone else driving me to the airport and leaving me at my drop off point. I had no choice but to leave the car and take my chances because we were running out of time. Once I got the baby and Teresa out of the car, I'd abandon it.

I looked around me to see if anyone or anything appeared dangerous. Honestly, I didn't know what to look for, but nothing seemed suspicious. I grasped the handle of the rear door and pulled. Teresa sat upright, her eyes filled with fear. They widened at precisely the same time I felt a hard body press up against my back.

"Hand me the keys."

I had no choice. If I made a scene either the baby or Teresa could get hurt. I couldn't risk it. The keys were in my hand. I turned my wrist toward my back and passed the usurper my keys. "I'll pay you more than Manny is if you let us go."

My comment was met with a laugh. "Your flight is about to leave. You'd better hurry."

In a heartbeat, I gasped, turned, and met kind eyes. Teresa didn't care about explanations and quickly got herself and the baby out of the car. She looked at the man, surprise registering in her expression. "Alejandro," Teresa whispered. She looked at me. "He works in the kitchen. He's a friend of Roberto's."

Roberto!

I didn't understand why Roberto or this man would go out of their way for us unless it was something I'd recently become familiar: compassion. Although I'd always been civil to Roberto, I'd never been what could be considered kind. The only reason I could think of that would motivate him to help was that, perhaps, his hatred of Manny was stronger than any indifference he might have felt for me. I wasn't sure if I'd ever know the truth. What I did know was, if I made it out of this alive, I had the means to reward his loyalty and would gladly do so.

I moved behind Teresa as we both walked quickly through the airport doors. I scanned the crowd, my eyes constantly roaming, holding my breath as I anticipated Manny or his men intercepting us at any moment. Thankfully, the line through security wasn't long. I staggered behind Teresa until three people were separating us. If Manny or his men did spot me, I planned to divert them away from the baby. If something happened to me, I was confident Teresa would get Eliana to safety once she reached the States.

"Passport and boarding pass." I handed the man both as had Teresa. Though I hadn't given it a thought, Teresa had looked at them in the car. She'd read aloud our aliases and said that Roberto had given us each a new driver's license for added protection.

The man looked at the documents and then at me. "Enjoy your flight." I went through the metal detector and quickly grabbed the diaper bag. Looking up at the monitor, I saw our flight listed.

"We have fifteen minutes," I said to Teresa. Eliana was still fast asleep, like a little ragdoll. I could only hope we hadn't given her too much of the medicine, but for now, I was thankful she slept.

Teresa and I flew through the airport as if we had wings on our feet. To avoid suspicion, I'd put on comfortable clothing and running shoes, and had left my hair hanging down straight. Pulling it forward over my shoulders and toward my face, I hoped to avoid notice. I wore no makeup, and my prescription eyeglasses, which I never wore in public, were perched on my nose.

Teresa wore flats and had a scarf tied over her

head. Both of our jackets were understated and simple. We'd put a knitted cap on Eliana's head, tucking her hair inside so no one could see the color. Her head laid over Teresa's shoulder. We'd also tossed a light blanket over her from head to foot. Hopefully, no one would recognize her.

Nervously, we approached the gate agent. She smiled at Teresa. "Ma'am, is your child under the age of two years?"

"Sí," Teresa answered.

The agent placed her phone under the scanner to read the boarding pass. *Ding* "Enjoy your flight."

Teresa quickly went down the gangway with the baby. Thankfully, the gate agent barely looked at me as she scanned mine. *Ding* "Enjoy your flight."

I hurried behind Teresa. Because we were so late for the flight, there wasn't a line of people to get on the plane, but once onboard we saw that there were limited seats. I scanned the aisles, and then bent over Teresa's shoulder and whispered in her ear. "There are three seats toward the back—one on this side, two on the other, same row."

She nodded, and we both walked toward the back of the plane. I followed behind, holding the diaper bag in front of me so as not to hit the other passengers and get noticed. When we reached the rear of the aircraft, I tossed the bag into the overhead compartment. Teresa was about to take her seat when my gaze settled on Eliana. I reached for her.

"Please, let me take her." Teresa smiled and nodded as I lifted Eliana from her. The poor woman had held her in the same position for so long, she rubbed her arm once I removed the baby. I held her close as I adjusted both of us into the seat. Scooting down, I moved the baby so she'd be sitting in an upright position, leaning against my chest. I placed one arm and then the other over her midsection, resting back into the seat. Pulling her close I utilized the remaining time we had together to hold her. I laid my chin on her head. She felt sweaty, but I dared not take the hat off until we were in the air. Someone might notice her—the wrong someone.

"Soon, princesita," I whispered, "you'll be safe." I touched my lips to her head and placed a soft kiss on her tender skin. I had one more thing to do.

Pulling one of the disposable cell phones from my pocket, I took advantage of the few moments I had left on the ground to activate it. I jogged my memory to remember the number of the only person who could help us, and the moment we landed I intended to call him.

Chapter 33

A^{ria}

The alley was narrow, the evening sun casting a shadow that bounced between the cement buildings. It was a secluded area, except for the back entrance to Miconi's Pizza on the next street and was much quieter than I'd expected. This team was a well-oiled machine if ever I'd seen one. They worked quickly and efficiently. If it weren't for seeing it with my own eyes, I would have doubted there was adequate space for these six hulking men and two blacked-out Humvees.

The effect that watching all of this had on my psyche was surreal. Never in my wildest imagination would I have thought to link these brawny men to my sweet, little daughter, and yet, here they stood. They were my baby's pumped-up, foul-mouthed, scarred, and tattooed guardian angels.

I smiled to myself as I watched them load the back of the vehicles. One by one they neatly packed bags filled with gear, and as I stood there, I said a silent prayer. Though wings were the last things I would ever suggest to Falcon's team, they had earned them just for agreeing to the mission. Without anyone other than Falcon knowing us, there wasn't one of them unwilling to blast through the gates of hell to bring our girl home. Now that I'd met them personally, not only did I believe they were entitled to those wings, but I believed that they deserved halos as well—tarnished as they might be.

Falcon came from behind Declan and me, outfitted in black boots, fatigues, and a black tee shirt. Since I'd only known him in a social setting, I'd never seen the intensity with which he carried himself until now.

Falcon tipped his chin up to the silver haired team member. "Ace? Your team ready?"

"Just about." Ace picked up two bags from the ground. "One more bag of gear and we're ready to go to secure the asset."

Asset. I didn't like that word.

Something inside of me warned that I should have been intimidated to approach the man but, surprisingly, I wasn't. Ace might look like he ate nails for breakfast but the past few months had made me equally as tough. With determination in my step, I walked over to the two big lumps of man flesh and wedged my way between them. They were hulking giants compared to me, at least as far as height was concerned, but I was sure I was just as fierce. I was confident I, too, could cut out the heart out of the person who hurt my daughter—and do it just as quickly.

My finagling positioned me so that Ace was now in front of me, with Falcon at my back. With arms firmly crossed over my chest, I locked eyes with Ace and gave him a stern look.

"I'd like you to stop calling my daughter an asset. Although I know in your lingo that's exactly what she is, to me she's my little girl. She has dark hair and blue eyes and likes me to sing to her at night. When she laughs the whole room lights up, and when she smiles your heart melts. I don't like her being called an asset. It's impersonal. It makes her sound like something you pick up at a hardware store. Her name is Karas. K-A-R-A-S."

I stood firm as his expression sobered, noticing that the corner of his right eye twitched as it narrowed. I hadn't noticed until then, but I'd been a bit louder than I'd intended. All the men stopped talking, and as much as I hated being the center of attention, I had to make a point. My nerves were raw. It didn't matter that I understood the burden of the mission, but I wanted them to think of her as something other than an asset, a target, or any other object. She was a person.

Falcon said nothing, still looking over at Ace for his reaction. With one arm crossed over his chest, he rubbed at the stubble on his chin with the other hand. I never tore my eyes away from his, prepared that I might receive a challenging look that was tough, hard, or menacing. I didn't. Instead, he nodded, giving me a look of sympathy and understanding.

"How about 'Operation Princess'?"

I felt a grin caress my cheeks as it spread my lips wide. Happy images flooded my mind. "She's quite the little princess."

Ace winked at me. "Then Operation Princess it is." He looked around at the group and raised his voice. "That good with you dipshits?"

"Yup." There was a bevy of baritone voices, each a staggered confirmation to their team leader.

I reached out, barely touching Ace's hand. "Thank you."

He looked to and fro, noting which of his men would dare eyeball him. When he was satisfied that he had only my attention, he winked again.

I turned and walked over to Declan. "Operation Princess," I said with a little more satisfaction than I intended. I was feeling a little less sick to my stomach and a little more powerful than I had moments ago. As if we'd choreographed it, our arms went around each other at the same time, his at my shoulder, and mine at his waist. He pulled me in close, and I felt safe, leaning on him for added strength. We'd get through this, and when every stone was overturned, and Karas was found, we'd hold our baby girl and never let her out of our sight again.

Carter came to stand with us as the men were seating themselves in the vehicle, when Mike Harris came stalking out of the back door and cupped his hands around his mouth. "Cap!"

Ace's head snapped around.

"I've got something!" Harris hollered.

The engines shut down, and the doors opened. One by one the men followed their leader over to the man in charge of information technology and intelligence.

Declan's phone rang. He looked at me and shrugged. He pulled the cell from his jacket pocket and held it up to his ear.

"Hello?"

As I looked at Declan, all color drained from his face. Carter noticed it too. Declan looked at his brother at the same time Ace looked from Harris to us. Declan's arm fell to his side, the phone now gripped in his hand.

"Who was it?" I asked, as Ace and Falcon marched toward us.

His expression was blank as he looked down at me, slumping over as if someone had punched him in the stomach.

"It was Marisol."

Chapter 34

Having arrived at JFK in New York, I had no idea what to expect. Traveling incognito was the norm for me, but this time it was a matter of life and death. I was terrified, that at any moment, Manny would have someone hurt us. That some sleaze-ball or crooked cop associated with my husband would take us into custody. If that were to happen, there would be no justice because sentencing would be dictated according to the law of Manuel Vallega, but so far I had eluded him. He would never think to look for me in a three-star hotel, dressed the way that I was.

When Manny and I had left the United States, I was highly recognizable. Not so tonight. I looked nothing like Marisol Franzi and I felt nothing like her either. Inside these everyday clothes was Marianna Vallega, and she in no way resembled a fashion icon. I felt like I was changing. The evolution was quick and I credited that to Eliana. Her presence in my life had expanded my thinking, causing me to stretch and examine everything I knew myself to be. Where Marianna and Marisol had been one woman, self-absorbed and self-centered, I had begun to separate the two. Slipping into Marisol's skin was easy. All it took was a change of clothing, hair, and make-up, but Marianna was more complicated. She was foreign to me. Her transformation was taking place on the inside. Whitewashing a blackened heart was much more work than I was used to, but then nothing in my life had ever been easy.

It was the inside of me that had changed. Where once I was fearless, I was now fearful. Although we were so close to achieving our goal, we were still miles away from the finish line. Anything could go wrong, but my primary concern wasn't for myself. If Manny caught me, he would kill me merely to rid himself of a complication. What I feared was that he would kill Teresa and the baby, or worse, and Manny's personal methods of dealing with difficulties were always worse than death.

I looked out of the window of the hotel room. New York City never slept. Memories of carefree days spent here filled me with a mix of emotions. I had more money, clothes, and shoes than I needed, yet still, I always wanted more. When was enough ever enough? I knew the answer to the question, and the one who'd taught me had a very limited vocabulary.

I pushed one side of the darkened drapes toward the middle of the window, leaving the other side open part of the way for light. This day felt longer than any other I could remember, and its toll was evident as I looked over at Teresa and Eliana. They both slept in one of the two queen-sized beds. Having slept this much, I was sure Eliana would be wide awake tomorrow. If I'd told Declan where we were, I was convinced he would have come tonight, but for Teresa and I that wouldn't have been a smart plan. Instead, we would meet him in Times Square tomorrow.

Of all the talents I possessed, conniving and strategizing were not the ones I expected to save my skin this time. Not only did I want to deliver Eliana safely, but I also had to protect Teresa. She was devoted to me, a fact I had blatantly disregarded until now. And then there was Roberto. He, too, had shown a loyalty I didn't deserve. I would reward them for their efforts—if I got out of this without prison time.

My plan was to meet Declan in the morning in the middle of Times Square. I'd told him no cops, no Feds, no wife. I couldn't accomplish what I needed if Aria were hurling accusations and taking verbal retribution as I exchanged Eliana for a safety deposit box key.

I'd told Declan the code to the lock on the door of my condominium. I'd long since given up the gratis one that Bella Matrix had provided for one of my own. I'd told him exactly where to find the key. If all went as I hoped, I'd get the key, go to the bank, get what Teresa and I needed, and be out of New York and on our way to Italy before nightfall. If things didn't go well for me, I wanted Teresa to go without me. She'd paid more than enough penance by being with me in this lifetime.

Emotion fell upon me, an occurrence that was happening more often as the days passed by. These were my last hours with Eliana. In just a few months this little girl had tipped my world off its axis. I didn't want to let her go, but I had to. My heart ached when I thought of never seeing her again, and I couldn't do that to Declan. There was a time in my life that someone else's feelings wouldn't have mattered to me. I was indifferent to how my actions affected anyone else. As long as I got what I wanted, I could sleep at night. But this little girl—an angel, really—had performed a miracle. She made me know what love felt like, and now I could never go back to the way I was before. She had used her innocent charm and pierced my heart, making it bleed. She was magical, and someone was trying to destroy her. I knew that this one act of redemption wouldn't absolve me of my sins, but it was a start. I might have been a cold-hearted bitch, but even I couldn't steal a baby from her father.

At one time Declan and I were friends, or I'd thought we were. I could only hope he'd understand I had nothing to do with kidnapping his daughter and that I'd risked my life to return her to him. Maybe we could be friends again one day. I hoped so.

Teresa had awoken and come over to the chair in

which I was sitting, looking down at me with kindness in her eyes. "It will be okay, yes?" I didn't answer because I didn't have one.

She patted my shoulder as I looked over at Eliana. "You need sleep. Go." She tipped her chin toward the baby. "I'll sit here. You go to sleep."

It was humorous how, now that we were in the States, Teresa only wanted to speak English. Though it was definitely broken and was seasoned with a Colombian accent, she was doing better than I would have expected.

I had tucked one leg under me to get more comfortable, but as I stretched it out pins and needles assaulted me. I limped over to the bed like an old woman. Behind me, I heard Teresa quietly laugh as I slid into bed beside the baby. With the pillow tucked beneath my head, I watched Eliana as she slept. She was on her back, and I gingerly placed my hand on her stomach. In her dreamlike state, she reached for me. As my eyelids grew heavy, her tiny little fingers folded around the side of my hand.

Chapter 35

Manny

A room at the St. Regis was the best that Manny could do on such short notice, but at least he was in New York. If he knew anything about Marianna it was that she was a creature of habit. He'd sent men out to scout for him, the first of three had just returned.

"Well? Did you go to her condo?"

"I did. There were two women living there. They said they were given the condo as compensation in their contract with the modeling agency."

Shit! It must have been one of her perks with Bella Matrix. He hadn't entertained that possibility, and he had liquidated all of Marianna's real estate holdings when he obtained guardianship. She could be anywhere.

It was late. Marianna wouldn't be foolish enough to be walking around New York City with a baby and an old woman. Not only would it be dangerous as the hours passed, but it would also be too obvious. She was slick, he would give her that.

Manny poured himself a drink from the bar. The suite was well stocked, and he needed something stiff to take the edge off. These last two days had been a shit show. The last thing he'd wanted to do was come to the States—especially after that bitch Kate Frampton's press conference. He could just imagine the Feds now, trying to connect all the dots to make a case to arrest him. Thank God he kept his lawyers well paid.

"Did you ask these girls if Marisol Franzi had come to the condo? Maybe Marianna hadn't realized the agency would take the property back and give it to someone else."

"I did. They said that she hadn't come by. I gave them the number to my cell and asked them to call me if they saw her. I slipped them each a thousand."

"A thousand?" Manny huffed. "That's nothing to those girls. If they're even half as good as she was, they make that in an hour." Manny flopped into a chair. He took a generous gulp of his drink and sat it on the table beside him. As he stared ahead, deep in thought, he ran his index finger around the rim of the crystal rocks glass. The sound it emitted seemed out of place, too eerie for such a lavish room.

"Maybe she went to Miami? You said that she likes Miami." The man was grasping at straws, but anything was better than waiting for Manny to explode.

Manny chewed at his bottom lip, never looking at the man as he mulled over his thoughts. "I don't think so. Marianna feels connected here. This place gave her her first taste of independence. You can't easily dismiss that." He thought another minute and then shook his head as he stood. "She's here. I can feel it."

Just then, two more men entered the suite.

"Anything?" Manny waited patiently, but neither had a look that said they'd found something.

"Sorry, boss. I went to a bar where I was told the models liked to go and asked about her. No one really knew what she was up to. When I asked if they could direct me to some of her friends they laughed and said, 'whoever told you that Marisol had friends?' and then they walked away and joined a bigger crowd."

Manny nodded, tension tightening his lips. He tipped his chin to the remaining man. "And what about you?"

"I couldn't get anything. Crazy as it sounds, I went to the major hospitals, thinking she might have taken the baby there to drop her off and leave, but I got nothing. I did pay off a few EMTs, cops, and security guards to let me know if she shows up, 'cause, you never know."

Manny raised his brows, surprised. "That was good thinking!" He held out his glass to the man. "Real good thinking." He swallowed back the remaining contents and then put the glass down on the bar's surface.

The men never took their eyes off him. His moods

had been more than mercurial the past two days. To look away might mean a bullet.

With hands in his pockets, Manny walked the perimeter of the suite, stopping occasionally to peer out the window. "I know she's here somewhere. It's just a matter of time until we find her."

The men sat and Manny paced, no one altering what they were doing, and no one spoke. It didn't matter how tired or hungry they were, they all waited for Manny's instruction before moving a muscle. Finally, Manny's cell phone rang. He walked over to the bar, having tossed the phone there when he'd put down the glass.

"Yeah?" To the men listening to one side of the conversation, Manny sounded as tired as they felt. "Oh, really?" His expression changed. A smile played at his lips, and his brow raised and furrowed. "That's good. Real smart. You did good. Keep me updated if you hear anything else." He hung up and slid the phone into his pocket. He folded his arms across his chest. Wearing a Cheshire grin, he rocked back and forth on the balls and heels of his feet.

"Good news, boss?" one of the men asked.

"Yeah. No hits on Marianna's phone, but I didn't realize we were still getting pings on Declan Sinclair's. Seems Marianna's got a meeting in the morning." He looked over at the last man who'd reported to him. "I need you to go back to the hospital."

Chapter 36

Aria

"Let's go over this one more time, Declan." Ace, along with Carter, had gone over the plan twice. I imagined they thought the third time was going to, indeed, be the charm.

"Meet Marisol at the designated spot. Make sure it's my baby and not a decoy. Hand her the envelope. Take the stroller. Walk away." Declan recited in monotone, then looked down at his chest. "Is this really necessary?"

Carter's even stare would have silenced anyone else but had never worked on his brother. "Yes. We'll be able to hear your conversation with Marisol. Once you give her the envelope, we'll be able to track her. That cute little keyring that we put on the safety deposit box key has a GPS tracker."

"Then what?" Declan pulled the tee shirt over his

head. Without unbuckling his belt or unzipping the zipper, he tucked the bottom of the shirt into his jeans. It was apparent he'd lost weight.

"Then we follow her, see who she's working with, and take her into custody. Kidnapping is a federal offense."

I found Ace's graveled tone comforting. Declan and I had been going around in circles with local authorities, bogus sightings, and dashed hopes. These men, as abrasive and intimidating as they appeared, were the first real source of promise we'd experienced. Appearances could, most definitely, be deceiving.

"Here, missus."

Lost in my thoughts, I hadn't noticed Henry Ford approach with a cup. "No, thanks." My stomach was a jumble of nerves. Any little thing that went wrong could affect Karas. I had no desire to eat or drink a thing.

"It's chamomile. Calms the nerves. It was over there on your coffee bar." His voice was soft and his manner even softer. Such a contradiction to his appearance. He pushed the cup toward me, his wanting-to-be-helpful expression urging me to do as he asked.

I took the cup from his hands. "Thank you, Henry."

"You don't have to drink it all, missus. Just a little. Might help."

"If you're done playing nursemaid over there, maybe you can get your ass in gear and your head on the fucking assignment." Ace's expression was one of impatience. Together with Henry Ford, Falcon was the only other member of the team that remained.

"What are the chances something could go wrong?" Declan addressed the question to Falcon.

"There's always a possibility that the mission could fall short, but the probability on this one is low." He moved closer to Declan with a single step to assure their conversation was a little more private. Henry Ford and Ace busied themselves gearing up. Handguns and Kevlar vests were all I could see, and the rest I didn't want to know about. Now that Declan was wired with a transmitter, he and I were an afterthought. I leaned in to hear Falcon, not wanting to miss one word before all of this went down.

"I give you credit for holding it together, when I know that you're chompin' at the bit. Hell, she isn't my kid and I want to punch something right now, but that's the rush, brother. We're all feeling it. We want to get in, kick some ass, get the bad guys, and get home, *but* not until we're sure your girl is safe." He looked at me, a mischievous smirk on his lips. "Besides, my wife would kick my ass if I didn't get her goddaughter home in time for supper on Sunday."

My bottom lip quivered, but I fought back my feelings. If these guys could *kick ass* as so eloquently expressed by Falcon, for my daughter, I could kick my emotions to the curb. Feel the fear and do it anyway.

There would be time enough after we all got home to indulge in feelings—and maybe a few beers.

"Ready, Cap. Let's go kick ass for Karas." Henry Ford smiled at me, knowing, in his own, weird, macho nursemaid kind of way, I needed a mantra.

"Kick ass for Karas," Falcon said with pride in his tone. "That's a pretty good one Ford. I like it."

"Me, too." Another whiskey-laced baritone chimed in. Ace almost had a smile on his face, and I just about fell over.

Henry smiled, obviously proud of himself for making two bulldogs crack smiles.

Within a few minutes everything that needed to be accomplished was complete. Falcon put his phone to his ear. "Zero eight thirty. Let's roll."

I suspected that was the order for the team as everyone made a single file line toward the door. These hotel rooms were not made for men this size. A hand came down on my shoulder.

"You're going to stay here." I spun around. My head snapped up. It was Carter. "The hell I am!" Everyone froze.

"Aria, it's safer here." Declan pleaded with his eyes.

"I don't care. You are NOT going without me. Absolutely not—or to say it your way," I looked from one man to the other in the room, "Abso-fucking-lutely not! I'm going, and you'd better not try to stop me!"

Chapter 37

Declan

Declan's senses were operating on overdrive. As each foot hit the pavement, the reverberation traveled up his legs, through his torso, and landed with a thud in his head. The fragrances of the city braided together, creating a putrid scent. He pushed down the contents of his stomach, most of which was coffee. The bitterness swirled in his esophagus, coming up when it should have been going down. The resulting headache from all of this was monstrous.

He didn't know who was where, but he knew they were there. Four massive beasts of men ready to help him get his daughter back. "Operation Princess" they'd called it. It couldn't be more fitting because she was his princess.

Another ten steps toward Times Square. The text this morning was from an unknown number. All it said was "TKTS." Marisol was smart, he would give her that. Even in the morning, the TKTS booth was crowded with visitors to the city trying to snag a bargain ticket to a show. He only hoped this went smoothly. Too many innocent people could get hurt if things went awry.

Wearing dark Wayfarers, he scanned the area. No sign of her yet. As he turned the corner on Forty-sixth and Broadway, his apprehension grew. He saw the black van on the street with its blinkers on. Falcon was standing outside of it talking to a cop, no doubt someone he knew. The ruse was supposed to be a broken-down delivery truck.

Looking up he saw a large, magnetic sign for "Le Fleur Florists" on the side. The back windows were blacked out, and the passenger's side and front were tinted. Somewhere behind that window was Aria, watching and listening as the events unfolded. At least he knew she was safe inside with Ace.

Declan crossed the street, just above the George M. Cohan statue. On a typical day he would have worried about jaywalking, but today he was just worried about staying alive.

Was Manny in on this with her? Would they use the baby as bait to kill him? Stop overthinking! Just stop!

It took all of his concentration to focus. Speculation was a sick merry-go-round, ready to whip your head around at breakneck speed. He didn't need that today. He needed to stay on task. He needed closure. He needed his daughter.

From the corner of his eye, he saw a huge man in a baseball cap with a Starbuck's cup in hand and recognized Henry Ford. Internal laughter came out as a snort when he thought about what was in that cup. After this morning's scene with Aria, he wouldn't be surprised if it was a Vanilla Chai Tea Latte. Ford was a good man, though. So were the others. Ace and Falcon assured him there would be someone around a hot dog stand, one near a Starbuck's—probably Ford—one who had his back, and one nearby. That was good enough for him.

Declan passed the van and headed for the meeting point. The line was long at the TKTS booth, which wasn't surprising. He scanned the space. No fucking divas with babies this early in the morning. He walked to the middle of the line. "Excuse me. Just need to get through."

An older gentleman and his wife took a step back. "No trouble 'tall," the man answered. "We're hoping to get Hamilton tickets."

Declan smiled at the man. His wife—or he guessed it was the man's wife—smiled sweetly, her rosy cheeks bright pink against her fair skin. He didn't have the heart to tell him that they didn't have a chance in hell of getting those tickets.

Declan stopped about four feet away from the line, in a more open space. Small groups of people dotted the small plaza. Some were consumed with chit-chat. Others had maps in their hands, and while one looked at the map, someone else scouted the direction of their destination. Looking down he noticed that his shoe was untied. As he bent down to tie it, the drumbeat in his head picked up a beat. No wonder. His pulse was pumping so hard it was a wonder he didn't burst an artery. This was a mistake. A big, fucking mistake. No way Marisol would risk herself for a little—

"Excuse me."

Declan looked up. The sun was in his eyes, shining directly over the shoulder of a jogger. He stood up, his vision no longer hindered by the direct rays. He thought it might be Marisol, but this woman was too plain.

She slid her sunglasses down her nose a half an inch. That was when he noticed the stroller was behind her. She said nothing, just held out her hand. She was waiting for the envelope.

"I—" Declan started to speak, but she put her fingers to her lips. He was afraid not to obey because his daughter's safety was at stake. Walking backward, she took a few steps around the stroller until she was on the side of it, the handle jutting slightly in front of her hip. With her index finger, she directed his gaze downward. He would have to move back a few more steps because his vision was hindered by snapped, side flaps.

He would never have guessed this was Marisol. As

he stepped back, he never took his eyes off of her. Three steps back. He placed his hand on the side of the stroller, determined that if Marisol were to make a run for it, she wasn't getting away with his daughter. His daughter!

The thought distracted him, and his eyes went from Marisol to the stroller. As he peered down into the seat, he grew dizzy. His knees wobbled. His vision splintered because the sun had exploded into bright, golden sparkles. He reached into his pocket, but before he could get the key out, Marisol had reached in with him and discretely pulled on the envelope, sliding it into her jacket with no one the wiser.

Karas reached for Declan's hand. Down on one knee, he held onto the side to steady himself with the other. Karas, laughing, bounced and grabbed his.

"I'm sorry. You have to believe me." Then she turned and ran.

Declan sprung up, not letting go of the stroller, but helpless to chase Marisol. It had happened so quickly. He didn't recognize her, so why would anyone else? They didn't know her. The only other people who might know were Carter and Aria and they were inside the tr—Aria!

He twisted the stroller around. He was chasing behind Marisol and Aria was running toward them.

"ARIA!" Declan ran, pointing at the woman running ahead of him. "MARISOL."

With her husband's shout, Aria's gaze deflected to

the side—and then she saw her. The evil Pandora who'd unleashed her box of abomination on everyone she loved.

Aria's pace doubled. Though she was much shorter than Marisol, she was also faster. She darted around people as Marisol tried to outmaneuver her. One was no match for the other. Aria grabbed Marisol by the jacket, and she spun around.

"I'm sorry, Aria. It wasn't my—"

The powerful force of Aria's fist met Marisol's nose, causing blood to spurt through the air. "Save it, bitch."

Chapter 38

A ria

Blood ran over my knuckles, but I wasn't letting go. I knew it was only a matter of seconds before Ace and his men arrived. The people in the square closed in to see what all the commotion was about. My hand hurt like I might have broken something, but I didn't care. I fisted Marisol's hair, wrapping it around my hand twice, and looked up to see my husband making his way through the crowd.

"Aria!" I couldn't see clearly because the crowd had closed in, but then I saw what he was holding onto. As my gaze traveled down, oxygen whooshed out. I fell to my knees, my free hand flying to my throat. *Karas!*

"Oh my God! My baby! My baby!" The words rushed out as a happy cry. Henry Ford came up behind me.

"I got her, Missus. Go get your—"

BANG

BANG BANG BANG

Complete chaos erupted. People started screaming and running for cover. I hit the ground with a thud as Henry Ford used his body as a shield and threw himself over me.

"Declan!" I screamed his name. He'd taken Karas out of the stroller and was holding her when the shots rang out. I could only lift my chin but saw Ace running Declan and Karas to safety. I looked over at an old man crying, hunched over his wife as he patted her hand. She was lying on the ground, a blank stare in her eyes while blood spilled from her abdomen.

Suddenly, I was in the air, my feet initially dragging. I quickly regained my footing, noting that Falcon had arrived to help Henry Ford take me to safety. Sirens blared. People rushed away from the square.

We came to a stop at the back of the van. The doors flew open and as I tried to jump up, Henry pushed me inside, nearly sending me airborne. He hopped in behind me and slammed the door closed. The contrast from sunlight to dark stole my vision. I heard, rather than saw, Falcon jump into the driver's seat. He threw the van in gear, his foot falling like a sledgehammer on the gas. The van bucked and jerked in his efforts to assure our safety. I tried to right myself as I was lying on my hip. I grabbed for anything that would assist me as my eyes adjusted to the dim light.

"Declan? Where's Declan?" My voice betrayed me. My mind began to race. Panic and anxiety dug pointy claws into my brain as adrenaline exploded through my system.

"Mama?"

What? What was that?

"Mama. Mamamamamamama."

Oh my God! "Karas? Karas? Baby?"

My heart stopped as her words trilled in the air. I heard her voice and time stood still. I'd missed her. I'd dreamed of her. I'd begged for her to come home.

"Where are you, baby?" I cried as I voiced the question. I grabbed at the air. My sight was clearing, but not quickly enough. From black to gray as the hazy veil lifted from my eyes and my vision returned to twenty-twenty.

"She's here, babe. On my lap." Declan laughed as I cried.

The mother in me leaped high into the air before hurdling back down to earth, only to burst into a million rays of indescribable bliss.

I scrambled forward as tears and the sweet face of my precious baby filled my eyes. Her smile split her face into happy pieces. I didn't care that the van was hitting bumps and potholes as I scrambled toward my girl.

I steadied myself against Declan's bent knees as he struggled to contain our most precious treasure, but as soon as I reached for her, my princess fell tumbling out of her daddy's arms and into mine.

Chapter 39

C arter

CARTER SPOKE with the local police as the EMTs assisted the wounded. Among them was an older woman, a twelve-year-old boy, and Marisol.

Marisol had been struck twice, and both entry wounds were from behind her. The gunshots came from the side of the plaza. Marisol was lucky. If Aria hadn't decked her, the trajectory could have been deadly. As much as Carter wouldn't have minded not having Marisol on the earth, Aria coldcocking her—well, he would have paid good money to see again!

As it was, Marisol was going to be out of commission for a while. One of the bullets hit her hip, probably breaking the bone. The other, they estimated, grazed her lung. Carter wouldn't know the full extent of her injuries until she arrived at the hospital and could be fully evaluated. For now, the EMTs were finishing up stabilizing her for transport.

So far, none of the cops had a clue who the gunman was. They were still canvassing the area for evidence. Carter's money was on Marisol's husband for two reasons. One, he had a gut feeling, and two, if Marisol were his wife, he'd definitely be tempted to shoot her. He made a mental note to talk to Ace when he got back to the hotel room. His guy, Mike Harris, was good at all that cybersecurity shit. He could weave in and out of the dark web. Eventually Manny and his slimy cohorts would have to come up from the bottom for air, and when they did, the Feds would have plenty to work with.

Right now, Carter had a job to do. Dig a little deeper and tidy up the situation. That was one of two things he was good at: clean-up, reconnaissance was the second. The X-tinction Force was a division of MarSin Falcon that, on paper, didn't exist, yet it was something he could see growing. Criminals were getting smarter and bolder and, to them, no one was untouchable. Falcon and Marc were taking the company in the right direction. Now that he'd seen one of their operations up close and personal, he wanted in. Too many scumbags were roaming the earth, and from what Marc and Fal had told him, the government needed them. No politician in a freshly pressed white shirt wanted to get dirty to keep the country clean.

Carter looked around Times Square. It was the very definition for the term "bright lights, big city." So pretty with so much corruption hiding in plain sight. He bet he could throw a quarter in any direction and get a handful of pickpockets, whores, and drug dealers. It was definitely time to expand the business.

"We're ready to transport her to NYP, sir."

The ambulance containing Marisol was within eyesight. The top lights were flashing, and they were ready to roll. The only thing left to be done was for one of the EMTs to secure the back door.

"NYP? Is that New York Presbyterian?"

"Yes, sir. They're waiting for her."

"Keep an eye on her. I'll meet you there. I want an officer outside her door. We'll need to ask her some questions."

"Not a problem, sir. They'll have her in the ER. Maybe in surgery by the time you get there."

He should have been elated. Jumping for joy. The woman who'd injected his life with so much pain was finally apprehended and, eventually, justice would be served. But he felt nothing. He issued the man a somber smile. "Thanks."

The sirens wailed as the ambulance drove out of sight. He was about to call his brother when he saw he had thirteen missed calls and about as many messages from Aimee. She was probably worried sick. That was the last thing he wanted. He hit the redial button and put the phone to his ear. She picked up on the first ring.

"Before you get your panties in a wad, Aimee, I'm fine."

A rush of air on the other end meant a sigh of relief. It was the first thing he heard. "I needed to know you're okay. That's all."

Damn, he loved hearing her voice. "I'm a big boy. I'm fine."

"Yes, and I worry. I can't help it. That's what happens when you're the wife of a cop."

"Retired cop," Carter corrected.

"Remind me who said he's on to bigger and better things." Amusement lit up her voice.

Someone called out for him and a cop was waving him over. He pressed the phone to his face so she could hear him better.

"Babe, I gotta go. I love you."

"I heard. Just be careful, and I love you, too."

Hearing her say it got him every time.

He slid the phone back into his pocket and looked around for one of the cops. "Someone said they needed me?"

"Yes, sir. This lady." One of the young guys, probably a rookie, brought over a lady wearing a worried look. "She's been asking for Mr. Sinclair."

Carter looked the woman over. She was pretty for

her age. Petite with dark, almost black hair mixed with gray. She wore it in a bun on top of her head.

"How can I help you, ma'am?

Her eyes brightened. "You are Mr. Sinclair? Mr. Dee-clan Sinclair?"

He laughed to himself. Her little accent was cute, but his brother probably wouldn't appreciate someone mixing the two of them up. He was the pretty one. "Sorry, ma'am. That would be my brother. Can I help you?"

She was instantly bothered by the news. A troubled expression twisted her features and shadowed her eyes. She was holding two envelopes in front of her. They looked a little worse for wear because of the way she was clutching them.

"Ma'am, if it helps, I'm going to see my brother in just a little while. Is that for him?"

"His name—Dee-clan Sinclair—written. See?" She held up one of the envelopes.

"Where did you get that?" He pointed to the envelopes.

"There." She pointed to the ground.

It had to be the envelope that Declan was supposed to exchange for Karas. Carter held out his hand. "I'll take that to him. Thanks for returning it."

She struggled for a few moments, seemingly looking him over to decide whether to trust him or not. Once satisfied, she handed the appropriate one with

Declan's name written on the front to Carter while placing the other in her pocket.

"Thank you."

Carter smiled. He liked her accent. Latin, no doubt, but her voice was nothing like Marisol's. Hers was light and sweet, where Marisol's always sounded bitter. "As soon as I see him. Promise. It'll be the first thing I do."

She smiled, nodded, and smoothed down the front of her coat. "Thank you very much. Goodbye."

She turned and quickly hurried away, making Carter chuckle to himself. She said "very" like the word "berry."

He had one more call to make before taking off for the hospital. Most everyone was where they should be, the cops having roped off the area with crime scene tape. No doubt it would be there through the evening.

"Dec?"

"Yeah?"

Carter noted that Declan's tone had lost its gravity. In its place was a lighter, fresher one.

"How's Karas?" He could hear squeals of baby laughter in the background mixing with some very deep voices.

"I'm sure you can hear her," Declan laughed. "She's charming the pants off these crusty fuckers."

"No worse for wear, huh? That's our girl. I can't wait to hold her."

"You got it, man. See you when you get here."

Carter nodded. "Will do. Some old lady dropped off an envelope for you. I'll give it to you when I get there."

"What old lady? Where? An envelope?" Declan paused.

"Yeah. Want me to open it?"

"Sure."

With his brother's permission, Carter slipped his finger under the edge. It wasn't fastened tightly. He pulled out the contents, gave a quick look, and then turned over the paper.

"Shit!"

"What?" Inquisitive and impatient, an edge smeared Declan's tone.

"It's from Marisol."

Chapter 40

M arisol

As I LAY on the ground, I tried to recall events, but everything was fuzzy. I moaned as I tried to move, but my arms wouldn't budge.

"Ma'am, we have your arms belted in for your protection. Please remain still."

What happened? Declan has the baby. I told him I was sorry. I wanted to tell him about Manny, but I had to get away, and then . . . and then . . . and then Aria punched me. Oh my god. There's a burning sensation in my shoulder. Like a hot poker. My chest hurts. I can't breathe. I can't breathe!

"Ma'am, please stay still."

My lungs are in a vise. Gripping. Stealing my breath! I have no defenses. Oh, my hip! It burns!

"Ma'am, if you don't stay still, I'll have to give you a sedative."

I hit the ground. I scraped at the tile. Cigarette butts and soot gathered under my nails. People were screaming. Everything was warm. The devil smiled at me.

He's taking me!

He's taking me!

Orange, red, and blue lights.

Blink

Pixelated images

Blink

The colors drained from the sky.

Blink

Men. Blue pants, white shirts.

Blink

I'm floating.

My gaze dropped, and I saw I was on a stretcher. Although I was very tired, I tried to take in my surroundings. There was a tube in my arm that led a trail up to a bag of intravenous fluid. Tape was on my arm and wires were on my body. A warm blanket was covering me, but I could see where the cables connected to the machines. Both monitors were beeping. One was soft and one sounded buzzier, but the tones were out of sync.

"Am I going to die?" I turned to the man on my left. My throat was parched, my words labored.

He didn't answer me. I tried to concentrate. Maybe he didn't hear me. I listened for more sounds. Four distinct inhales and exhales in the silence. There were people in the back with me. I turned my head to look behind me. Two people were in the front, but still no one answers me in the back.

"Am I going to die?" I swallowed what spittle I could muster, rolling my tongue around to try and wet my mouth. When I licked my lips, they stung, but they were a little numb. Still, no one answered me.

Panic started to set in. I felt nauseous.

"Please. Help me. If my husband finds me, he'll kill me."

Someone touched my head to ease my rising panic. It was somewhat comforting because I was so tired. So, so tired.

I tilted my head toward the person petting me. There was something about their cologne. It was spicy. Musky. Familiar.

Oh, God!

I tensed. I tried to scramble out of the restraints. *This can't be happening!*

"Hush now, Marianna. I'm not going to kill you. I have *other* plans."

The End

Keep reading for a preview of

Boundless Hearts: A ROCK HILLS Origin Story, now available at your favorite bookstore.

254

Preview of Boundless Hearts

Author Skylar Harrison spends hours writing love stories for her many readers, leaving little time for her to write a real-life love story of her own.

Dash Barrows, lead guitarist for "BOUNDLESS HEARTS," is at the top of his game and the charts. Women are easy to find but not love, leaving him jaded.
A serendipitous encounter turns the lives of two strangers upside down, leaving them breathless.

When fates collide, does time stop, or has the wheel been spinning all this time?

BOUNDLESS HEARTS is the origin story for the series ROCK HILLS.

Keep reading for an excerpt.

Prologue

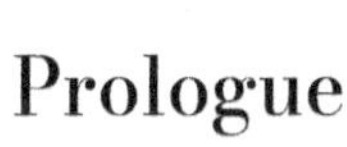

April 15, 1912

"Don't be afraid, Abby. Just look at me."

There was no madness in Isidore Eisenberg's eyes, despite the chaotic circumstances. His tone was calming, something his wife desperately needed. She was shaking, the motion rattling her body all the way to the bone. Abigail didn't know if it was from fear, the cold, or a combination of the two, but her husband's sweet words tucked around her like a warm blanket. It was the only comfort she could feel.

"Do you think it will take a long time, or that there will be much pain?" Though Abby asked the questions, she wasn't confident she genuinely wanted the answer. It would take however long it would take; there was nothing more they could do. The outcome of their circumstances was bleak, at best.

As the couple lay side by side in the darkness, Abby tried to think of something on the bright side. She could only think of one good thing about their current situation, that they were together. She wasn't a brave woman. Though she hated knowing her sweet husband, Izzy, shared her fate, there was a part of her that was grateful she wouldn't have to face the horror of death alone. She looked into her loving Isidore's eyes, knowing full well he read her thoughts.

"Now, Abby," he said as his hand brushed her cheek, "don't worry, my love. This situation is something we can't control. We must look forward. Our time after today will be an eternity, dearest. What we're going through—what is happening right now—is a temporary inconvenience. We've always known death was a certainty, we simply never knew when it would come. And isn't this exactly what we'd hoped for? To be in each other's arms until the end of time?"

Abby nodded. Her husband always spoke the truth, and today was no different. From the day she'd married him, Abby had told him he was her life, her breath, and her destination. On that beautiful June day, she'd also promised to stay by his side for the remainder of her existence. By the end of today, her promise would be fulfilled.

An eerie whine was followed by a loud bang, causing the iron bed to shift. Muffled screams in the distance carried through vacant staterooms and hallways and found their way to the couple in cabin C-26. The sounds were frightening, immediately bringing to mind how quickly their impending fate would come to pass. Fear flooded Abby's veins with adrenaline. Her body jolted, every limb reacting to what she knew was in store. Death.

Though she quickly tried to hide her reaction and regain her composure, Isidore noticed. He knew her so well. Sadness veiled his gaze, a look Abby couldn't remember seeing in all their years together. But a solution for this disaster wasn't within her husband's control, nor was any of it of his making, for if Izzy could have changed their circumstances, she had no doubt he most certainly would have. He squeezed her hand, lassoing her torturous thoughts to capture her attention.

"Abigail, do you remember our second date?" His voice was hoarse, and his teeth chattered, yet he put on a smile for his beloved wife.

"Of course I do, but our first date stands out equally as well. Don't you remember? Our first date was a disaster."

"Yes. It was a pitiful excuse for a picnic," Izzy laughed. "My gallant attempt to chase the ants off of your skirt caused quite a ruckus—and captured the notice of everyone in the park!"

"Of course, it did! As the bugs fell off my skirt, they scrambled up my legs, and you went under my shift after them. It was scandalous! Imagine if you'd seen a young man putting his head up our daughter's skirt. I can't even fathom it!"

A broad smile hooked the corners of his mouth. His lips were perfect. They were plump, but not like a woman's. They were entirely masculine. Whereas some of the women Abby knew tried to keep their husband's advances to a minimum, she'd welcomed every kiss her Izzy had shared with her these past thirty years. Abby hadn't known much about life and men when they first married because she'd been but a girl. Still, from that very first night spent in Izzy's arms, he'd played her body as expertly as a finely tuned instrument, bringing it to life.

Their life together had been magical. The two enjoyed everything about each other. Abby especially loved her husband's touch. His simple, tender acts warmed her heart, and sex was a pleasure, despite her mother's instructions that she wouldn't enjoy that particular wifely duty. Her alone time spent making love with Izzy had never been a chore. Even at this age, and for as long as they'd been together, they'd done so often, sometimes more than once a day.

Though, for some, that might seem scandalous, Abigail relished the feeling of her husband inside her. The skin-on-skin connection was something she'd come to cherish. Remembrance of those times made her realize that stolen moments such as those would be no more, and the thought made her suddenly feel lonely.

Melancholy breezed through her mind. Elsewhere in the world, this night would play out very differently for a vast number of couples. Those lucky people would have hopes and dreams intermingled with rapture, where, instead, theirs would be, quite literally, drowned in grief. Where others in the world would enjoy touches and kisses holding promise, Abby and Izzy's would end with a final goodbye.

A shiver possessed Isidore. His arm shook as he tried in vain to control the reaction and hold Abigail close. She shifted, turning on her side to ease his discomfort. Pain and stiffness resulting from the frigid atmosphere only allowed her to move an inch at a time. She refused to let it deter her, and she moved, albeit slowly, to allow herself what little comfort she might find. When she had finally settled, they were so close that barely a breath separated them. Abby was drained from the small effort, and Isidore trembled from the cold. The lids of his beautiful, brown eyes fluttered, his dark lashes lingering on his face too long, freezing against the skin above his cheekbones. Abby knew that if she didn't keep him talking, he would fall into a deep sleep, never to awaken.

She spoke to him, not willing to let him go just yet. All that Abby needed was to hear his voice, even if it would be for the last time. She snuggled close, gently nudging him. Her voice was barely audible as the freezing temperatures strained her vocal cords.

"Izzy, why did you ask if I remembered our second date?"

His eyes slowly opened. Even though he was exhausted, her sweet husband responded to the sound of her voice. He'd done the same when they were at home. He always had. Abby was never an inconvenience to Isidore, and, for that, she was grateful. Unlike their counterparts, her husband never behaved as if she were an obligation he had to tolerate. Every single day of their married lives, Isidore gave his wife the best of himself, never what was left of his time at the end of the day.

"Our second date?" Izzy paused, his memory was taxed, and his gaze thoughtfully traversed the blank space above them. Slowly he recalled asking the question just a few moments before. Abby traced over his forehead with a gloved hand, a gesture she'd repeated many times before, allowing her thumb to trail across his skin, lingering on the furrowed lines of his brow. "Ah, yes," he croaked. "I remember now." His concentration had given him another few moments of clarity, and he looked deeply into his Abby's eyes.

"By the time of our second date, my fate was sealed. You claimed me."

"Me?" Abby's question was laced with surprise. "What did I do?" She coughed as her trembling hand moved down his face and palmed his cheek. Izzy pulled her closer and held her tighter, the action causing a pained expression on his face. His eyes, however, reflected nothing but tenderness.

"It was your eyes, Abigail. They enslaved me. On our first date, they drew me in—those beautiful baby blues." He cleared his throat, his gaze turning a bit more serious. "However, it wasn't until our second date that my poor heart bore the brunt of their impact upon me. Your gaze branded my soul. I knew by the end of that evening I never wanted to spend another day of my life without the pleasure of looking into them every night. It was that day I decided we would wed. I was determined to do whatever was necessary to make you agree to marry me."

Abigail's heart broke beneath the sincerity of his words. "Oh, Izzy!" A sob clutched her throat. The impact of their circumstances made her want to cry, but it seemed that even tears were denied her in the Arctic atmosphere. "It seems so cruel we've been robbed of our future together. I'm jealous of those that will survive this. It's maddening to think we planned our lives so meticulously, and now our careful preparations to enjoy the rest of our days won't come to fruition. I don't want this to be the end. Despite your high opinion of me, I am, admittedly, a selfish woman. I want more time with you."

Izzy gave his wife a tender smile. "As do I, my dearest, but we are not the controllers of our fate. One day at a time is how we measure our happiness, and even that we aren't promised."

Suddenly, the ship lurched, nearly catapulting them from their bed. A cruel, pain-filled shudder attacked Isidore as a piece of their luggage skimmed quickly across the rising water and slammed into his back. Abby opened her mouth to scream, but no sound escaped as Izzy's head snapped back from the impact. She quickly gained her composure, knowing their time was limited. She was terrified he'd been knocked unconscious, and what few, precious moments they had left, might have been stolen away by the collision.

"Izzy!" Abby's voice was panicked and hoarse, her cry a mere croak. "Izzy, please don't go! I need you."

Though the action was delayed, Isidore gradually opened his eyes. Relief flooded Abby as she gazed into the warm brown orbs that had anchored her through her entire adult life, and, though weak, she offered him a smile. Tucking her arm around his waist, it instantly locked into place due to the bitter cold.

"I'm not going anywhere without you, Abby. Hold onto me. Look into my eyes. Let the fear fade away."

Always the obedient wife, Abby did as her husband requested, anchoring herself in the love reflected in the warm, brown pools. It was the only heat between them. The piercing and penetrating cold had caused the blood to drain from his handsome face, leaving only a frosty remnant of his natural, healthy color. There were things to say, tender thoughts that needed to be voiced, and only this moment to express them.

"My sweet, sweet man. I'll say the same words to you now that I said the day we married. You are and have been, my life, Isidore Eisenberg. As I think upon our journey together, I have not one moment of regret. With my last breath, I want you to know that I am, still, desperately in love with you.

Her confession warmed his heart, and Izzy knew that they had, at best, moments to say their final words to each other. "I'm so sorry, my dearest love. This trip was supposed to be an adventure, not our end, but it's only one of the many destinations you and I have shared. It seems our next journey will, hopefully, be to heaven. I won't grieve, because at least there we'll be together."

Tears wouldn't come, but the effort stung the corners of Abby's eyes. A sudden movement made her flinch as a sloppy, frigid wave splashed atop her woolen coat. It triggered a layering effect starting with outer-wear and then causing the skirt beneath it to quickly saturate with wetness. The heavy material slapped against her skin, so cold that it burned. The seawater was littered with chunks of ice, the pieces now quickly closing in on them as it rose above the top of the mattress. Abby trembled, terror clobbering her with the same ferocious impact as their ship when it hit the iceberg.

The room pitched at a near ninety-degree angle, and the bed catapulted into the wall at their feet. Again, Abby tried to scream, but dread clutched her throat, squeezing away all sound. She was terrified she would be torn apart from her husband and launched into open space. Sensing her fear, Isidore grabbed her with whatever strength he had, seizing any precious moments they might have left. In a flash, the water was around their necks, then chins, rising quickly to just beneath their mouths.

"Abby. Look at me."

Panicked, Abby looked one last time into the eyes of the man who had always made her feel safe and loved. Her quickened breaths burned her throat and chest, fueled by fear. They had seconds, at best, to share one last breath. Isidore had managed to squeeze out a final tear, and with blue lips and chattering teeth, pressed his lips one final time to the woman who would forever own his heart.

"Don't be afraid, my love. We'll be together again. Look for me. I promise; I will always find my way back to you."

Chapter 1

"**D**ear sweet baby Jesus! Do you think any of these people know to cough into their elbow instead of sharing their cooties with the rest of us?" Skylar Harrison mused aloud as she ground her teeth. She had little patience for stupidity. A self-professed germaphobe, her skin crawled every time someone sneezed in her direction.

"I know, right?" Skylar's friend and editor, Vincent Mannon, snapped back a retort as he sighed. He sat in the seat right beside her, sharing Sky's silent hope that their next stop on this business trip wouldn't be to one of those express medical centers for some antibiotics.

Sky huffed and nodded her agreement. She hated business trips, but they were a necessary evil for a journalist, and her work had taken her all over the world. She'd accomplished much, delving into the heart of her stories and describing them in such detail that many publications clamored for her work. *Time* magazine had featured her latest piece. Vince was convinced a Pulitzer was in her future, having witnessed the effect Skylar's stories had on her readers. He encouraged her to continue writing in-depth articles, but Skylar was now working on her third book as Eden Skye. Her goal was for her novel to hit the trifecta of bestseller lists, *USA Today*, the *New York Times*, and the *Wall Street Journal*.

Using her real name and reputation, she could quickly have done so. Instead, she'd adopted a pen name and was publishing her books independently. Once she accomplished what she'd set out to do, she planned to use her experiences in a series of articles. The world of self-publishing had upset the control traditional publishing houses once held. Amazon had opened a new world to those with vivid imaginations, and she planned to chronicle every detail of her experience and report what she found on her venture.

"I'll be right back." Vince left his backpack on the ground, giving Skylar a smirk as he approached the Cinnabon counter. A few minutes later, he returned, the proud owner of one of the giant, sticky pastries.

This wasn't anything new. Vince had a wicked sweet tooth and indulged it whenever they traveled. The airport kiosks were the perfect excuse for a treat, tempting and teasing even the most adamant dieter with savory sights and smells. Skylar followed Vince with her eyes, her judgmental expression having no effect on him as he returned to his seat with the sugary confection in hand.

"Don't you have diabetes?" She gave him a disapproving look.

"I do, but I take insulin." He shrugged. "Don't judge me."

"I'm not." Her statement was weak and flat.

"Yes, you are. It's not like I do this every day. Besides, I didn't eat breakfast," Vince scolded in a hushed voice. When anyone, especially Skylar, pointed out health concerns related to his glucose level, he became irritated. As far as he was concerned, his blood sugar numbers weren't anyone's business but his own. Besides, life was too short not to indulge in tasty food.

Just to spite her, he held the sticky roll in the air and moved it slowly toward his mouth, making a full display of taking that first, sweet bite. He then closed his eyes, enraptured as the sweet taste hit his tongue. When he opened them again, he smiled devilishly at her as he chewed.

Skylar rolled her eyes, turning away. It was too early to be goaded into a discussion about the benefits of a healthy diet. Instead, she reached down, unzipped the top of her laptop bag, and rummaged around for a pencil. Vince had his obsession with sweet things, and she had a thing for mechanical pencils. She loved them and purchased a pack nearly every time she went to stores like Target and Walmart. Pencils were forgiving. Their erasers permitted a person to make mistakes. What she didn't like were pens. Everything about them was too final. If she made a mistake with a pen, her OCD dictated she rip out the page and start all over again. No one had time for that nonsense, and that was what made pencils the number one choice of perfectionists everywhere.

"What are you writing?" Vince peered over Skylar's shoulder, making her pull her work a little closer to her chest.

"Nothing, nosey. Just looking at your edits."

"The edits are done." His tone was flat. "Move on to the next book." The hair on the back of Skylar's neck bristled. She didn't take orders, especially from someone on her payroll. There was a way to voice his opinion nicely, but Vince rarely did so.

"That isn't me, and you know it. I always re-edit when I get my stuff back." The monotone statement was one she'd delivered many times over. How long would it take for people to understand the luxury of being an indie author? Control. Skylar would always have the final say on her work as long as she published independently.

"I get what you're saying, but you have to ask yourself if it's the best way to use your time. That's why you pay an editor."

She rolled her eyes, partially because she knew

Vince was right and, also, because she knew she should let the story go and move on to the next in the series. There was a vast difference between writing an exposé and writing fiction. The characters' lives she created were entirely at the whim of her imagination. There was only one problem, she became attached to her characters as she developed them. As she grew their personalities, they became as real to her as the man sitting beside her. It was hard to let them go once they were published. Not so with a piece for a magazine. Those were facts. This was fiction.

She ignored him, reaching into her bag once again to find a notebook. Vince's expression held a question. "I'm fleshing out the next story. I'm not exactly sure where I want to take it."

"So just get your thoughts down on paper and let me do the rest. Use your imagination, and I'll polish the words. You can't drag your feet, Sky. There's too much competition."

Though he spoke while chewing a mouthful of food, her disapproving look wasn't lost on him. He put his hand in front of his mouth to be polite and kept right on talking. Thankfully, only two more bites, and he'd be finished.

"This is really delicious. You should try one." He mumbled the words, pausing a moment to swallow. As he brought a napkin to his lips, he wiped away the flicked remnants of white icing that remained.

"Excuse me."

Skylar and Vince simultaneously looked up. The man sitting directly across from them broke in on their conversation. He had his laptop in front of him while he worked at one of the airport computer stations. Apparently, he'd been listening as they talked.

"I couldn't help but overhear you talking about edits and rewrites. Are you an author?"

His expression was sincere, his eyes gentle. Skylar was instantly drawn to the rich, velvety sound of his words. Some men were famous for their voices being their most prominent feature. This guy could have capitalized on that attribute.

"I'm an editor. She's an author," Vince replied. As expected, her editor's welcoming delivery and friendly mannerisms drew the stranger in.

"I'm sitting here working on a story. Do you mind if I ask you a few questions?" He gestured to his laptop, then returned his attention to Vince.

As expected, Vince saw the potential for a new client and didn't hesitate to engage. "Not at all. What can I help you with?"

As the two men continued their conversation, Sky tuned out from the world, turning back to her notebook. She had no trouble ignoring people around her and could completely disengage when necessary. It was a skill she'd mastered at an early age. She was an only child and a bookworm like her mother. Her early love of reading had taught her how to make observations and write the details within the scene. She was then able to transport herself into the stories she both read and wrote. Everything around her faded away in the distance as she immersed herself in a book. She'd traveled the world, fallen in love, and experienced heartbreak, all in her imagination. Her reader base for the new pen name was a faithful one. Although she'd created the persona of Eden Skye, she found she liked being Eden. It freed her to write romance the way she felt it should be. Sky took her obligation to the readers seriously because they fell in love with the people and places in the worlds she created, just the same as she did.

"Sky, are you going to answer him?" Nudging her with his elbow, Vince interrupted her thoughts.

"Huh?" She looked between the two men, confusion clouding her eyes as heat flushed her face. A prickling sensation raced up the back of her neck, the evidence of her embarrassment at having ignored them.

"Sorry. I wasn't paying attention. What was the question?"

"What kind of books do you write?" Again, the man's tone caught her attention, caressing her ears with much the same velvety effect as James Earl Jones, Alan Rickman, or Patrick Stewart. She loved voices, especially rich, deep ones. Skylar would eagerly listen to any of them read the daily newspaper and never lose interest.

She looked up at him, a smile filling her lips.

"Romance. Contemporary romantic suspense, to be more specific."

"Ahhh. Romance." He exaggerated the phrase and bobbed his head, acknowledging her chosen writing genre with a crooked smile.

His expression wasn't lost on her, his was the response of many people when telling them she was a romance writer. She detected a hint of disapproval or condescension in his voice. Instantly, she felt the need to document his reaction with all the others she experienced for the exposé she had planned. Though he would never note the difference, her thinking morphed from romance writer to investigative reporter. It would only take a matter of minutes to tell if he was genuinely interested in her as a person or humoring her because he didn't take her work seriously. She took mental notes whenever the subject arose. What she'd discovered so far was that those on the outside of the romance genre dismissed love stories as nonsense. He would be shocked to know how many indie romance writers had healthy bank accounts.

She inclined her head as blood simmered in her veins. "Yes. Romance." The answer was defensive and clipped. It seemed she was always defending the choice to write love stories. She'd met people like him before. Judgmental. Quibbling about the content of romance novels. Everyone had an opinion. If the story was too sweet, it was judged as not realistic. Too erotic, and it was "mommy porn." She hadn't invented the chip on her shoulder; it was put there by the patronizing attitude of people who didn't even read the genre.

Really, what was the harm in escaping to love and passion within the pages of a book? She believed there was none at all and dismissed those with negative attitudes for something they knew nothing about.

Having been put in a position like this before, Sky stood her ground, trying hard not to be rude. It was more like digging deep, planting her feet in the statistics of how many romance books were sold each year. She prepared to state her position that, romance genre or otherwise, a writer was a writer regardless of content. "It seems I'm a hopeless romantic and write stories that, as a whole, generate over one billion dollars in sales per year." A disdainful smile was all she could muster for this asshole. She couldn't help but feel a little smug defending her career decision with facts. "So, you see? There's quite a market for love stories."

His eyes never left hers. She'd said her piece and readied herself for what would come next. Would he be an arrogant dickhead, or would he open his mind to something that was a little outside his wheelhouse?

She studied him, the moments ticking away as she readied herself to defend her position and that of the romance writing community. What she hadn't expected was the warmth she found in his gaze, and the longer they sat there, the more she found herself trying to resist the magnetism of the sweet, chocolate-colored pools.

Chapter 2

G rinning, he cocked his head. "What's your name?"

His deep baritone slightly short-circuited Skylar's concentration. He was a mystery that she planned to unravel. She chastised herself for forgetting her discipline as a reporter. She was supposed to stay impartial and not lose focus when investigating a story. His voice was at fault. It caught her unaware. She hadn't anticipated that something so inherently masculine would wrap around her like a fur coat and pull her in. She hadn't dated in a long time and, other than Vince, she didn't have too many conversations with men. Like a dry sponge, she soaked in the sound. The melodic tone sank into her muscles and bones.

Unfortunately for her, she didn't recover quickly enough for her liking, and her distraction cost her. The tight grip she'd had on her notebook relaxed. As her hand fell open, loose sheets of notes she'd tucked in between the pages tumbled to the floor, scattering everywhere on their way down.

"Shit." Immediately flustered, she cursed herself for the faux pas. She tried to snatch the falling jumble of creased loose-leaf paper and Post-it notes, attempting damage control. It was too late. While she grabbed at some of the fallen items, she experienced the domino effect. Her arm bumped into her laptop bag. That, too, tumbled, spilling even more of her things to the floor.

If there had been a hole nearby, Skylar would have crawled into it. She looked anything but ladylike as she tried to catch the contents. Half the bag emptied, and she wasn't quick enough to save the other half. She was embarrassed. Her laptop, flash drives, pencils, and various other contents went everywhere. But fate wasn't done with her yet. To add insult to injury, she knocked her fresh cup of coffee, sending the venti to the floor, the plastic lid popping off when it hit. It splashed everywhere, wetting the papers that had preceded it. She was mortified. Now, not only was the research and working copy of her manuscript on the floor but they were drenched. All this time Vince watched as the disaster unfolded. His eyes went wide. All she needed were some clowns and elephants to go with the circus.

"Shit, shit, shit!" Fumbling through her pockets, she grabbed the small pack of Kleenex that was hidden within. With only a slight handful to help her, she grabbed the laptop, dabbing at any liquid that could seep through to the keyboard.

It took a moment for her editor to regroup and, when he did, he popped out of his chair. "I'll grab some napkins." The urgency in his voice meant he sensed her distress. He ran off, but Skylar didn't see him. She was too busy expending her efforts to save the electronics before they fell victim to the coffee. All she could picture in her head was destruction. One soaked keyboard meant the laptop was shot.

"Here. Let me help."

Skylar responded to the outstretched hands, though she wasn't sure who possessed them. She shoved a handful of dripping paper into open palms. The hands were much larger than her petite ones, the fingertips thick and calloused. She grabbed her Kindle and an extended battery pack, as well as four or five flash drives, and handed them to the Good Samaritan. Through her peripheral vision, she saw they were being placed on the seat next to where she'd been sitting before she looked like a failed juggling act.

She reached for the leather bag, quickly shoving in the items that had fallen, but hadn't been hit by the coffee. She was flustered when she quickly stood. It was definitely the wrong move. The sudden motion triggered off a flash of vertigo and she lost her balance.

"Whoa!" She wobbled as she tried to catch herself, reaching out for anything that would stop the spinning, when someone caught her arm before she fell to the floor. The jerky motion nearly sent her spiraling again when she crashed into a hard body before she had a chance to go all the way down. The collision ignited sparks that jolted her so unexpectedly her eyes grew wider than silver dollar size. *What the hell was that?*

Slowly, Sky regained her footing, her balance normalizing enough to stand. She looked up to thank the person who'd stopped the world from spinning when they had so quickly run to her aid. Brown met blue. As she looked into his eyes, the buzzing continued, the hum of electricity growing stronger as she was drawn into their warmth. Fireflies fluttered low in her belly. She struggled to breathe, her chest tightening as she stood captured by his gaze. The feeling was exciting, but it frightened her.

Sky moved back to identify the intercessor who'd placed himself between her and the floor. *Oh, God! Mister Anti-romance.* He seemed to be in as much shock as she. As much as she wanted to turn away from him so she could shut down the power grid connecting them, she couldn't. A lock clicked between his eyes and hers. His pupils dilated, the gold flecks within like sparklers on the Fourth of July, in response to their contact. Though Skylar couldn't see her reflection, she was confident her own had responded in much the same way.

"Thank you," was all the response she could muster. Through reason scratched her thoughts with the idea of turning and walking away, a strange, invisible tether lassoed them. Two people knotted at the moment of contact. Sky could tell by looking into his eyes he'd felt the link and, suddenly, he didn't feel like a stranger at all.

She was more confused now than ever in her life. He smiled, studying her. His lips were full, and she couldn't shake the feeling she wanted to kiss them. The thought appeared out of nowhere, wholly unbidden and unwanted. Instantly, her gaze faltered. From one second to the next, her line of sight had dropped from his mouth to the floor. She found herself staring at the faded, grey carpet, unable to describe what was happening. Drained, she tried to think of anything other than what had just occurred.

"You're welcome."

His voice was as sinful as chocolate, and her cheeks as red as cherries. She couldn't look at him. She had no doubt his response was sincere, but too many things happening in such a short span of time had sent her into a panic—and she never panicked. Even if he'd been a temporary knight in shining armor, she was no damsel in distress. *But he did help to rescue the computer.*

As the small crowd around her zeroed in on the mishap, Sky forced herself to take in a lungful of oxygen even though she struggled to breathe. She didn't like being the center of attention, especially when air seemed to be in short supply. Helplessness didn't look good on her.

Grasping at mental straws, she made an attempt to regain her composure. She needed to calm the hell down and get ahold of herself. Had to pretend it was no big deal. It was critical she quickly adopt an indifferent air. Call up the few remaining, sentry-like brain cells she possessed and turn them into seasoned soldiers. At least maybe then she could protect what was left of her dignity. She inhaled slowly, taking in a deep, calming breath.

And another.

And still another.

Deliberately, she lifted her chin. The handsome man's gaze hadn't wavered. He was still looking at her, and that strange, fluttery feeling reemerged.

Feeling like an awkward teenager, Sky's stomach flipped. She looked away, feeling like a scared rabbit. Slowly she grounded herself, waltzing words in a melody of thought.

He's judgmental.

He's arrogant.

He's just a guy.

"Are you okay?" The stranger's voice skipped up half a beat as he hitched words to a smile, turning her insides to Jell-O.

"I'm good, thanks." She shrugged, wrapping an arm around her waist to get ahold of herself. It didn't take but a moment to shift the focus of attention away from her. As she collected her things, the people who'd been watching moved on, their attention drifting back to their laptops, books, and phones. She went back to her place, which now felt like the hot seat since Vince and the man changed seats. Now she was sitting directly across from Vince while only one seat separated her from her helpful stranger. She looked from left to right and, when she was confident she was no longer the object of everyone's attention, she attempted a casual conversation so as not to appear rude.

"Now that we've seen my method of researching for a novel, it's your turn. You and Vince were talking about editing." She leaned in his direction, pretending to peer over the empty seat at his laptop to see what was on the screen. "What kind of book are you writing?"

"Me?" He acted surprised as he looked at the content on his screen. "The great American novel, I guess. Isn't everybody?" The sound of his hearty laugh filtered through her, causing a pleasant sensation.

"Sounds like a best seller." She tucked away her earlier assessment of the man. Maybe she'd misjudged him. He seemed kind of . . . normal.

"Right. I've been writing this story on and off for years. I'll probably never publish it. It's just something I like to do."

She relaxed her shoulders, enjoying yet another mild jolt of electricity that his voice elicited. He didn't seem like an arrogant asshole at all. In fact, his smile made her curious. There was a bit of an edge to it. She couldn't decide if he was just playful or a wild boy.

As she sat back in her seat, he gave her a brief description of his novel. She wasn't listening. Instead, she studied his face—for research, of course. His cheekbones were high and noble, his jaw, square and strong. And then there was his voice. Whether he was a good writer or not, she couldn't tell, but with a voice like that he should have been a singer.

"You never know." Sky smiled. "Yours could be the next literary mega-hit. I mean, c'mon, look what happened to the lady who wrote *Fifty Shades of Grey*."

On a huff, his eyes closed, and his chin dropped. A minute later, he peered up, directing his attention to the screen of his laptop with a slight wave of his hand.

"What I'm writing has absolutely nothing in common with those kinds of books. Nothing at all. This is literature. Not erotica. It's complex. A period piece. A tale of discovery and grit. There's no kink in my story—or fluff."

Sky bent her resolve, giving him a narrow glance with a playful but deadly message.

"I think Ms. E.L. James might object to her multi-million-dollar babies being referred to as fluff. The only thing fluffy about the figures in her account are the clouds she floats on when she goes to the bank." Light sarcasm tickled her tone. "I guess I should add that the book we're talking about sold over one hundred and twenty-five million copies. And that was just the first book. It's part of a trilogy."

He gave her a knowing look, his smile never leaving

his face. "Have I offended you? I'm not trying to. I'm just stating the differences between a romance novel and serious literature. You can't compare *War and Peace* with *Fifty Shades of Grey*."

"I can if the sales are there." Her comeback was lightning-fast. "*Lord of the Flies*" sold a little more than twenty-five million. *To Kill a Mockingbird*, a bit more than forty million. And let's not forget the darling of romance, *Gone with the Wind*. That little gem—thirty million." She quirked a spunky brow. "You, sir, should know your facts and figures before you dismiss something of which you, clearly, have no understanding."

An impish grin wrinkled her forehead. She didn't mind defending her craft. Her bank account was nowhere near as healthy as E.L. James's, but she couldn't complain. Writing romance had proven to be a good career move for her, and no one could say she didn't have peer loyalty. Was he up for the challenge of a debate? Because she could play that game all night. She'd done her research.

The rumbled laugh was robust and thick. Deep and smooth, that luxurious kind of sound came from deep down. She shivered, then chastised herself immediately. She wanted to hear it again, so she asked another question.

"What part of the country are you from?"

He seemed surprised she'd changed the topic from books to places. *Oh, well.* She was one of those people who researched exciting subject matter for a living.

Everything from "Where is the best place to bury a body?" to "What R&B song is more births attributed to?" had been typed into her web browser. Like dandelions in a garden, topics just randomly popped up in her thoughts. It was her experience that, if she didn't immediately take care of the weed, it was determined to grow stronger until she did. If he was going to write a book, he'd have to research a hundred different topics at a time too.

"The Midwest, originally, but I've lived all over the country. Up and down the East Coast, then some time on the West. I've been back and forth, once or twice."

A stab of guilt hit her for having a combative edge in her tone. She wasn't trying to put him on the defensive, just have a conversation. *Oh, for God's sake!* The only way to fix this was to ease up. "So, where are you on your way to now?"

"Back to Florida. I'm in the middle of a move from Florida to Annapolis, Maryland."

The tactic worked. His expression was a little lazier. Relaxed. But a move to Annapolis from Florida? She didn't understand that logic.

"You're moving *from* Florida? Why would you want to do that? Winter's coming. Maryland is so unpredictable weather wise." Intrigue swept her expression as she silently questioned the sanity of a man who would choose bipolar temperatures over toasty ones. His shrug was indifferent. "Florida's nice, but, honestly, I'm tired of it. A few years ago, I took some time off. I honestly thought I would settle down there. It was only for a short time, I considered it semi-retirement."

"Semi-retirement? You're what? Thirty?"

He laughed at the surprise in her voice. "Yeah. There is that. You can only sit on your ass for so long, you know? It ends up being the same shit, different day—I was bored. And to tell you the truth, I really like Annapolis. I missed the change of seasons, and Maryland in general. It's convenient. Kind of in the middle of everything. Three hours one way, you have the mountains. A few hours in the opposite direction, you have the ocean." His hands went up as he mimicked a balance on a scale. "Beach in the summer. Skiing in the winter. What's not to like? You know, Land of Pleasant Living?"

She was sure she almost gaped. *Retired?* Out of their entire ten-minute conversation, that was the topic that piqued her interest the most. She could paint a house with all the speculations in her head. He was so young!

Wild scenarios danced the cha-cha in her thoughts, each question two steps forward, each answer, a step back. What was he? A lottery winner? Trust fund baby? Maybe she should give him the benefit of the doubt. Perhaps he'd invested better than most people his age. Money from a dead relative? Male gigolo? The possibilities were endless and were more than enough to keep her intrigued.

Now he really had her attention. What she wanted

to say was, "Are you crazy? Last winter was brutal. Three major snowfalls. You're nuts!" but decided she might appear to be the crazy one. Instead, she was polite.

"I think I would have stayed where the beach is warm and sunny."

He smiled a naughty grin. "I don't think it would have worked out for me, had I stayed in Florida."

"Really? How so?" Puzzled, she was anxious to hear the answer.

His brown eyes warmed in intensity, competing with the mischief tickling his lips. "Because, if I had, I wouldn't have met a nice girl like you."

Heat rushed up her neck and made a mad dash for her cheeks. Her lips made an O as surprise opened her mouth.

"You're blushing," he said. "And it's quite a pretty, rosy shade."

~

Boundless Hearts: A ROCK HILLS Origin Story is now available at your favorite bookstore.

DD Lorenzo is an award-winning author of Women's Fiction and Romantic Suspense novels. She loves coffee, long lunches with good friends, and fresh flowers to balance her obsession with anti-heroes. You can find her most days plotting and planning her character's lives from her beach house on the Delaware shore.

To stay updated with DD's books, please visit her website at www.ddlorenzo.com and sign up for her newsletter. Want the inside scoop? Join DD's reader group, DDs Diamonds, at www.facebook.com/groups/ddsdiamonds

Stay connected with DD

Website:

www.ddlorenzo.net

facebook.com/ddlorenzo.author

x.com/ddlorenzobooks

instagram.com/ddlorenzobooks

pinterest.com/ddlorenzo

bookbub.com/authors/d-d-lorenzo

amazon.com/DD-Lorenzo/e/B00GA5ARJ8

goodreads.com/D_D_Lorenzo

Other Titles by DD Lorenzo

The IMPERFECTION Series

No Perfect Man

No Perfect Time

No Perfect Couple

No Perfect Secret

No Perfect Woman

No Perfect Beginning: An IMPERFECTION Series Prequel

The ROCK HILLS Series

Boundless Hearts: A ROCK HILLS Origin Story

Bone Dust: Rock Hills Book 1

Standalones

Indiscretion

(An Aleatha Romig's Infidelity World Novella)

Heels, Rhymes, & Nursery Crimes

(A multi-author series)

Twinkle, Twinkle Little Star: Fragile Flower to Femme Fatale

www.ingramcontent.com/pod-product-compliance
Lightning Source LLC
Chambersburg PA
CBHW021038310726
48969CB00006B/1714